FRIENDS of the BRIDE

BY

B.B. Free

Binkwell

Though the settings in this book are based on actual places, the narrative is a work of fiction. Characters, names, businesses, places, and events are wholly fictitious. Any resemblance to actual persons, living or dead, or to actual events is purely coincidental.

Copyright 2020 B.B. Free

Book design and production by Dave Bricker

ISBN: 978-0-9861201-1-4

For John, the keeper of the dream

Author's Note

When my husband proposed, the circumstances were unusual, for this was merely the second time in my life in which I had managed to forge friendships with several women all at once. I spent a healthy amount of time with these women and shared an unlikely amount of personal information. They became an integral part of my journey from ring to altar. Although we are still a part of each other's lives in one way or another, the group has dispersed as our journeys have taken us on different paths, but for that brief, magical moment, we lived through the most pivotal time of my adulthood together. They are the muses who inspired this book, and although the characters quickly morphed into new entities and manifestations of different aspects of my own personality, each of these women lives in the protagonists of the story as do I.

As the book took shape and I shared the creative process with these friends, each one recognized and relished the character she inspired as well as the fictional roads taken, the decisions made, the lessons learned, the healing, and the personal growth. That said, I must state the obvious: This is a work of fiction. Names, characters, and incidents are the product of the author's imagination, and any resemblance to actual events or persons, living or dead, is *mostly* coincidental.

B.B. Free

FRIENDS *of the* BRIDE

Grace

W. C. Fields once said, "No doubt exists that all women are crazy; it's only a question of degree." I take issue with that axiom, but watching the frustration on Jack's face, it occurs to me that maybe Fields had a point.

"I don't get women. Your favorite sport is gossiping about each other, but if I dare make a comment to take your side, you pounce on me. I just never know what to say anymore."

Jack is my fiancé, and this is not the first time he's looked at me as if I needed meds. Jack is as wonderful as men can get. He is so smart, but his intelligence is simple—simple but elegant. He is reliable, measured when addressing others, committed, and oh so easy to get along with, but in me, God has handed him the greatest challenge of his life.

Most discriminating men would keep a healthy and wise distance from a woman like me, but not Jack. During my dark moments, I often wonder out loud what could be wrong with him for loving me, mostly to wound him and bring him into my gloom so I won't have to face it alone. But he never succumbs. The first couple of times it shook him a bit, but after he figured me out, he developed impenetrable shields. Good for him. I guess that's why he is relentless about putting a positive spin on my pessimism. He likes to say that surviving my so-called "calamities" gives me majesty, that my herculean yet useless efforts to let go of grudges make me lovely, and that battling against my instinct to be bitter keeps my spirit alive. He makes it difficult for me to stay in my dark corner.

Today has been particularly perplexing for Jack. I have just subjected him to a verbal dissertation on why I am mystified and exhausted from my latest conversation with my friend Maddie. Ever since she caught her husband cheating for the third time—with the same woman—and finally decided to divorce him, a big chunk of my life has been dedicated to comforting and reassuring her.

"I love her but I'm so tired of saying the same thing over and over. I want to ignore the phone when she calls late, but somehow, I just can't. I guess it's my fault since I did tell her to call me day or night if she needed me. Every time I want to hang up, she asks me the same question: 'Why, Grace, why did this happen?' And every time I get sucked into it again."

"Maybe she needs professional help."

"She says she's considering it."

"Well, between the wedding chaos and staying up late with her, you're not getting much rest lately."

He's right. Our wedding is less than five months away, and though it's as small as a wedding can get, planning a short ceremony and a dinner for two-dozen people comes with a surprising amount of stress and disruption.

"I know, Jack, but how can I not be there for her when she's helping me so much with the wedding?" I flap my arms in indignation.

"Okay, give her a list of counselors and shove her a little."

"That's awful! She'll think I'm trying to ditch her."

"Aren't you though … a little? You have things to do."

Jack, bless his heart, has the courage to support me. As thanks, I proceed to make a 180 and jump to Maddie's defense.

"You could do that to a friend? You're despicable."

"I'm despicable." He says it back to me slowly, almost as a question, his eyes narrowed, like he's trying to decipher the inner workings of my neurotic mind by reading my forehead.

Wow! No wonder he's backing away, with his eyes firmly planted on me (I guess for fear I will attack him from behind), scratching his head. I have turned a sophisticated, brilliant professor of music into a frightened and confounded creature. He should've gotten a German Shepherd instead of taking up with me.

I'm damaged, I know it, but I'm working on it. All those years of feeling as if I were outside of life looking in, as if I had worth only when summoned to provide this or that service for mom, or ex-husband, or daughter, or friends, must be the reason I took up residence in my steel shell. It's where I lived and where I thought I would remain. Now, during my "mature" years, I've been given the opportunity for a do-over. I have a successful although not high-paying professorship in the English department of my beloved South Florida College. I have a tender, devoted man in my life, and a small, tight, self-contained group of women who have been stitched into the fabric of my world and are slowly, almost imperceptibly, transforming it. It's a good life now. It's not perfect, but it's good.

I walk over to where Jack sits on the couch. The room is lit only by the light coming from the TV. Behind his glasses, I can see his eyes fixed on some cop show. I plop myself next to him. His concentration is unbroken. Or is he afraid? Like a forest animal that stays still, almost not breathing, when a predator is present. I'm the predator. I feel ashamed. Aren't girls supposed to be made of a perfect blend of sugar and spice? I've lost a lot of my sugar through the years, and most of what's left is face-slapping spice, but I'm working on it.

"Sorry, I don't make sense sometimes."

His eyes are still on the TV. I watch his folded arms rise over his chest as he sighs deeply, he stretches his long, lean legs and crosses his ankles. "It's okay, Grace." I love to hear him say my name. It's like warm sunlight on my face. And then, without looking away from the screen, he swings an arm around me, and gently brings me into the crook of his shoulder, where I fit so perfectly, as if Providence had planned it so before time began. It's where I belong. *I belong.* What a miraculous thing. Every time the thought forms in my mind, without fail, I get choked up. So, in the interest of not making Jack even more uncomfortable, I shake it off.

"Mark is not coming to the wedding." The volume of my voice is normal, so now he looks at me. He probably thinks Mr. Hyde is back to Dr. Jekyll.

"How come?"

"He's out of town on business that weekend—can't get out of it. You okay with that?"

Jack chuckles.

I envy how guys don't feel wounded when a buddy can't make it to an event, even a wedding.

"Yeah, I guess."

Mark is married to my college friend Daisy, who glides in and out of our "conclave" as Jack calls my group of friends, a sort of honorary member. One or two other women remain on the periphery, by their own choice, not ours.

"What about Lily?" he asks tentatively.

"She's not coming either."

"And are *you* okay with that?"

"I'm torn. Some days I wish she would come, and some days I prefer she wouldn't. I don't know if I want to deal with the tension. Is that awful to say?"

"No. It's understandable."

Jack and Lily, my twenty-three-year-old daughter, have an easy, loving relationship, and I suspect he'd like her to be at the wedding, but he always has my back.

I don't know if I would describe my relationship with Lily as complex or complicated. I'll call it *complexicated*—it's multilayered and oftentimes difficult. I raised Lily virtually by myself. Her father and I divorced when she was a toddler. At best, he had marginal contact with her during the early years; then he just faded away in a blur of excuses until it became too inconvenient for him to forge, let alone maintain, a relationship with her. This launched my obsession to create a stable environment for Lily, to set her up for success, and to show her father, and the world, that we needed no one. This attitude contributed greatly to my subsequent isolation from the sisterhood of human females.

I can rest easy knowing that I accomplished what I set out to do, but in retrospect, I can't deny it cost me dearly, and the price I paid was not worth it. Because you see, my zealous pursuit of structure and stability became a slow-spreading shadow that crept into every area of my life and, sadly, my daughter's. I stunted her growth.

"Mom, stop trying to make me into another you! I can't be you!" That sound bite plays in my head every moment of my life.

"I don't want you to be me." I rejected her accusations fiercely. "But I want you to learn from me. Why do you insist on making your life harder for yourself when I can help you?"

"Mother, please let me make my own mistakes. I won't learn just 'cause you show me. Let me just find my own way."

I think back and realize how frustrated and helpless she felt. But I wouldn't listen. My way was best, and I could not allow her to stumble through inexperience when I was there and willing to hold her hand and spare her. It didn't work. As soon as she turned eighteen, she bolted, and not on good terms. All the ducks I'd lined up for her she shot down, one by one, in her wild search for herself. She lost her full scholarship, dropped out of college, and still can't hold a job or pay rent long enough to put down roots. Our interactions are strained at best, with intermittent periods of estrangement. Oh, we go back and forth attempting to reinvent our relationship. We speak. We don't speak. I place her in the Almighty's hands every day and beg him not to make her pay for my arrogance. Guilt is my drug of choice.

But I'm working on it.

••

"This one is cute, don't you think?"

I notice Jo swallows hard and Maddie reaches for her cell phone, a telltale sign that she's repressing something.

"What? What's wrong with this one?"

Silence.

I turn back to the full-length mirror that reflects a forest of snowy gowns in this vast and intimidating bridal shop. I assess the white knee-length strapless dress with the light beading on the skirt, one of the few the store could guarantee to have ready in time. The consultant had a difficult time hiding her discomfort with the challenge of finding a dress for a wedding only five months away plus a bride with a modest budget and a less than model figure. "I think it's pretty, right?"

Crickets.

"MADELINE!" I try to bring her out of her stupor.

She looks at me and stuffs the cell phone in her purse a bit more forcefully than is customary. "It's a freakin' rag! I don't want you to wear a rag on your wedding day!"

"That's just a summer dress," Jo pipes in with a hint of her all-but-abandoned Brooklyn accent. It always comes back a little when she's making a strong point. "Take it on your honeymoon, but if you wear that to the wedding, every other woman there is gonna look better than you. That's not acceptable."

I'm stunned. How many times have we had this conversation? This can hardly be considered a proper wedding. It's just a little over twenty people (maybe), a simple sunset ceremony on a small private beach in the Keys, and a casual dinner. "One step above eloping," as Jack likes to describe it. Why do they insist on dressing me up for a royal event? Why don't they get it?

Mercifully, my mental pity party is interrupted by a flurry of activity in the vicinity of the store entrance. Sylvia arrives rushing through the long center aisle, leaving a scented trail of expensive perfume. She is completely oblivious to the fact that she has nearly knocked over an employee while trying to manage an oversized handbag, a leather laptop case, and a cell phone that is eternally attached to her ear. She refuses to get one of those Bluetooth gadgets that go in your ear because she says they clash with her jewelry, which always consists of pieces so exquisite they should require the services of a twenty-four-hour bodyguard.

"I'm so sorry I'm late." She hangs up and kisses us hello. "I just left the longest, most unproductive meeting. I told them my time was too valuable to spend on insipid ideas. If they haven't made some decisions about the layouts before I get back, they can all be replaced."

She sinks into an armchair, crosses her sickeningly statuesque legs that culminate in the creamiest Jimmy Choo pumps, and exhales away her annoyance. "So what did I miss? What's that you're wearing, Grace?" Her face curls as if offended by a foul smell.

I now look down miserably at the dress I thought was charming just ten minutes ago. I feel like Cinderella after her ball gown turned back into tatters.

"She wants to wear that dress to her wedding," Jo volunteers. Sylvia's eyes widen in surprise but just for a second, and she quickly recovers.

"Oh no, that won't do. Here, I brought some pictures from our summer brides' issue." She opens her handbag, pulls out her iPad, and instantly produces half a dozen pictures of white dresses in a variety of airy fabrics that seem to flow even in the stillness of a one-dimensional screen. I must admit some are quite fetching.

She shoots a look at the sales consultant nearest to us and places the gadget in her hand. "See if you can find anything like this, thank you," and she turns to us assuming the store employee is familiar with her iPad and quite sure that she is expeditiously carrying out her orders.

Another futile attempt at wedding dress shopping has thankfully come to an end. At this moment, I feel happily married to the lychee martini caressing my lips. We have reached détente in this cold war. I have agreed to continue the search for a long, flowy number, but what I haven't told them is that I have a safety net. My plan B may just be a white sundress I purchased last year at my favorite boutique, which happens to look quite handsome on me. What they don't know can't hurt *me*.

My unsolicited wedding stylists and I have been getting together once a month for nearly a year now to share in the one indulgence that is our common denominator: fine dining. Our individual financial profiles range from modest to affluent, but when it comes to scoping out the best places to eat, all six of us do whatever it takes to make it work. It helps having our own media expert. As founder and editor in chief of *Vivace Miami*, an elegant lifestyle magazine that covers all there is to know about our city, Sylvia gets firsthand intelligence on the where, when, and what of restaurant-hopping.

Fortunately for those of us on the modest side of the money curve, we decided on a little Miami Beach flavor tonight. Doraku is our favorite place for happy hour and sushi and sitting in one of the intimate booths makes me feel like an A-list movie star.

"So how was the dress hunting?" Mindy doesn't waste a minute upon taking her place at the table. She hangs her tailored jacket behind her and smooths a few flyaway hairs into her back slicked bun. My recess is over.

"Zero hits." I take a long, slow sip of my drink. "Where's Peggy? Is she coming?" Maybe I can divert the attention away from the dreaded dress topic.

"Yeah, she just texted me," says Mindy. "She'll be a few minutes late. Practice went long. So tell me, how'd it go?"

My dumb luck.

"I don't think this girl knows what she wants." Jo points at me with her long-nailed finger, which is sporting a large ring worthy of the pope.

"Ya think?" I serve them some sarcasm as I resurface from my swim in the vodka. "I was sure that was painfully evident."

"Why do you think you're having so much trouble choosing?" Sylvia squints as she attempts to dig into the psychological roots of my indecisiveness. What I would like to scream is that I thought I knew what I wanted until they all made this into a Svengali project. They're trying to build a bride.

I reluctantly place the martini glass on the table very close to me and leave two fingers straddled on the stem. This drink is my only true friend right now. I will try this one more time.

"I don't want this wedding to be a big production. It's important to me that we keep it intimate and focused on the significance of the day. Jack and I are not pretentious people, you all know that. I want it to reflect who we are. I want it … well, simple."

Looks bounce around between four sets of eyes like Ping-Pong balls. After a few seconds, Maddie puts her hand on my arm. "But sweetie, you're not simple. Your wedding invitation is written in Shakespeare's English and you read him for fun." She says this in a delicate tone, as if she were telling me that I'm adopted. Maddie is *aaall* sugar. Is that possible? Can a woman be that nice to all people all the time and be authentic? Maybe, but it's weird to me. She looks around for approval. Sylvia and Jo smile gently. Mindy nods. And then we all burst out laughing so hard, several adjacent tables can't help but join in although clueless as to why. Perfect timing for Peggy to show up.

"Hey girls, what's funny?" She's a little out of breath as she motions to the waiter. Her ash blonde pixie-styled hair is wet, and today, like most days, she's in athletic wear. This one has an elegant floral print in shades of blue and gray. She probably showered after practice and changed from a sweaty outfit into a fresh one. "Whatcha drinking, Grace?"

I raise my glass to her without a word.

"Ah, I see you're in the zone. Okay, I'll have one of those, please." The waiter retreats. "Well, I'm happy to report that Mackenzie's serve is now a lethal weapon. The hard work finally paid off."

I don't know where Peggy gets the energy to be a full-time tennis coach at the college and spend several evenings a week coaching Mackenzie privately. I'm tired just listening to her, but her blue eyes sparkle with excitement, and I'm glad for her.

"Woo-hoo!" We all cheer, myself the loudest, elated as I am to finally shift the focus off me. As our waiter elegantly lays our delicacies on the table, I take a second dip into my lychee martini, and say hello to my coconut shrimp. Like morning fog surrendering to the sun, my mood begins to lift.

"I really think this kid has potential. Guys, it's astonishing. The volunteers at the community center say he spends hours after school just looking off into space until I get there. As soon as he sees the rackets, man, he comes alive!"

"Why does he spend so much time at the CC?" Sylvia licks her lips after swallowing a forkful of spicy tuna salad.

"I'm not sure. He doesn't talk much, and I don't push him, but what I gather from the grapevine is that he lives with his single mom who works two shifts at a hospital cafeteria, and maybe she prefers him to be at the CC rather than home alone."

"Hmm … isn't he about seventeen? Why would she prefer him to have supervision? Something's going on there."

"Sylvia's got her journalistic groove on." Maddie winks as she plows through her tempura veggies.

Sylvia laughs between bites. "Yeah, journalist, sure!" Sylvia may be editor in chief of a lifestyle magazine, but she never forgets that she got where she is because of her work in photography, not her journalistic credentials. And she is successful because she is brilliant, especially at surrounding herself with aces in the field.

"There's more to this story, I know, and if I'm going to help him go further with his tennis, I'm going to have to dig a little deeper pretty soon. But I feel our connection is so fragile, I'm afraid one wrong move and he'll pull away." Peggy's eyes are fixed on her plate as if she's speaking to the salmon lying on it. "Plus, the fact that I have to start finding another place for us to practice, assuming he wants to continue."

"Why?" Mindy has been quietly absorbing the conversation, as is her nature, while enjoying her black tiger shrimp in that poised and deliberate way she has.

"Didn't you hear? Funding for the center is being cut off as early as next year. The private contributors aren't interested in continuing to back it, fund-raising has been miserable, and the city doesn't even want to hear about shelling out any money."

"Wow! That's sad. They have really good day care and seniors' programs there," Mindy says.

"Yep. Not to mention the youth program. I've been volunteering there for a few years now, and boy, they really stretch those dollars, so if they're talking about closing down, the situation must be really awful."

"How much money do you think they need to run it?" Mindy is fully engaged now.

"I have no idea, but they do a lot with very little, so I don't understand why their funding sources are turning away from it."

"I'm going to look into it." Mindy points at the air with her knife. "Maybe there's something we can do. Grace, you should talk to Ursula. She's always looking for charitable opportunities to get a tax break."

"Oh, she'd love it," I say. Ursula is one of those "satellite" members of the group, and she is indeed swimming in money. She is humble and genuine to a degree that is almost detrimental to herself, she is obscenely generous and cannot stand to see someone in distress of any kind. She made her money in a way that is unheard of in this millennium of quick stardom and easy wealth: She worked very hard for it. When I look at her, I have to resist the urge to bow to her.

Ursula came to the United States from her native Germany with two small children in tow to escape an alcoholic husband whom she feared would one day kill her or one of her babies. She refused to tell her family where she was to protect them, and for years didn't communicate with them. Those were lonely times. Calling upon the memory of an old friendship, she begged an ex-pat buddy of her father's for a job in his textile factory in New York. There, she found herself enthralled by the process of textile manufacturing. She researched, studied, and explored colors, textures, and qualities of fabric in the most exacting detail, like a cosmologist deciphering the behavior of heavenly bodies. A few years later, with the help of the old man, who had become her mentor, she moved south and opened a small store. She turned out to be a cunning businesswoman. She took care to offer unique and superior fabrics, and quickly became popular among the local up-and-coming designers cropping up in the growing Miami fashion district. Now, twenty years later, together with her daughter Tammy and son Frederick, Ursula is the CEO of her own multimillion-dollar international company that services top designers all over the world. That's why she seldom has time to wander around with us from eatery to eatery.

"I'm sure she'll want to be involved, but what about us, couldn't we do something? Maybe some fund-raising of our own?" I love a project.

"Okay, Grace, get on it, you're the big planner." Jo smiles and snaps her fingers in the air.

"I'll talk to Jack. No one is better at making money multiply."

"I could definitely work on creating awareness, spread the word, maybe even run an ad in the magazine, and get some press coverage, for sure." Sylvia swiftly takes over.

"I'll do whatever you want me to do as long as it involves baking." It takes a lot to get Jo this excited. I'm impressed. Her work as pastry chef at an exclusive hotel restaurant consumes her. Getting her to stray from her routine requires a minimum of two weeks' notice.

"Jo, we could make a fortune on your cakes alone," I tell her. "When Mindy gets the facts, I'll give it some thought. Maybe Peggy, Jack, and I can do some brainstorming with the college administration." Between the three of us we represent three departments, a significant sector of South Florida College: English, Music, and Athletics.

Maybe this is what I need right now to stop obsessing about all the wedding minutiae. Come to think of it, maybe this is what we all need, a way to redirect our attention onto something that will put this wedding into its proper perspective.

Peggy already burns with desire to help Oceanview Community Center, where she spends most of her free time anyway as a volunteer. Maddie is in desperate need of an escape from the swirling tide of her unsavory divorce. And for months, Mindy has been pondering over the importance of having a deeper purpose in life. Yes, I think Oceanview may turn out to be the lighthouse that gives us all some productive direction.

By now, we are so galvanized by this endeavor, as we often get when we embark on some new adventure together, that our dishes are getting cold and our drinks warm.

"Let's talk timetable." Sylvia takes her iPhone out of its holster, techy gunslinger that she is, to check her calendar. "We should set a date to meet and discuss whatever information and ideas we have so we can get the logistics together. The summer's going to be pretty busy for all of us."

And then, in a flash that jolts me out of my comfort zone just as I've dropped my defensive shields —

"And you Grace, have a wedding to plan."

Peggy flashes me one of her toothy, sparkly-eyed smiles. "Speaking of your wedding, how was dress shopping?"

Oh no! Not this again.

Peggy

•

I'm excited that we're finally moving forward with the community center project. I feel a sense of purpose I haven't felt in a very long time. This is coming at exactly the right time. I was starting to feel engulfed in monotony, and to boot, I can't shake the desolation I feel after last night's phone call to Penny, which triggered painful memories of our youth. That's not an unusual outcome after many of our talks.

I'm not that dense. She doesn't have to give me such a long menu of excuses for why I can't come for a visit. One will suffice. Or better even, tell me the truth. You don't *want* me to come.

It amazes me how my twin sister inherited my dead mother's skill for making me feel like an extra in the story of my own life. If Penny and I weren't identical twins, I could believe I was picked up from a trash bin. I'm so different from them. How did that happen?

Penny is prissy and eternally preoccupied with the latest hairstyles, fashion, and nail polish colors. The number of times in our almost sixty years of life that we played a sport together can be counted on the fingers of one hand, and most of those times ended abruptly because she broke a nail or didn't want to sweat.

I, on the other hand, am the anti-Penny. Putting on makeup requires a gargantuan effort and an extraordinarily important occasion. My hair is short and styled so I don't have to give it any thought other than to wash it, and the only question to answer when I shop for clothes is: Can I wear this to work and/or the tennis court, or volleyball court, or basketball court?

That is not to say that I haven't tried. Growing up, it was just the three of us after Dad died at the age of forty-one from a bewildering heart attack. I was eleven years old and the bottom fell out for me that day. Dad was always on my team. He loved me for me. He came to my defense time and time again when my mother became irritated because I wouldn't play with dolls or tea sets and fussed and worried because I read too many books. I wasn't like Penny and I didn't "play like a normal girl."

"Leave her alone, Pearl! Let her climb trees and run around the yard if that's what she wants. And what's wrong with reading books?" Then, he would take me outside, play hide-and-seek with me for a while, and walk me to the drugstore soda fountain for a Cherry Coke. On the way home, he would speak consoling words to convince me that I was beautiful, and smart, and that it was perfectly fine for me to like sports and books, and wear shorts and sneakers, and that not wanting to put bows on my head didn't make me a lesser human than my twin sister. Those moments when he soothingly nursed the wounds of my self-worth gave me the resolve I needed to turn a deaf ear to my mother's and sister's indignant objections when I announced one day, much later, that I would be going to college to get my degree in exercise physiology.

Dad was the thread that kept me connected. When that thread was severed, I felt myself sinking into uncertainty as I entered junior high. I had to hold on tight somehow.

And so I tried. I took a page from my twin's playbook and put on a Penny mask which looked remarkably like me on the surface. I wore dresses without complaining. I signed up for dance lessons with her. That was fun, though, and I was good at it. Athletics and dancing are very close relatives. I also joined my sister when she watched my mother go through the ritual of preparing herself for her frequent dates, which began uncomfortably soon after Dad passed.

But when we started high school, it all went downhill rapidly. Penny began hanging around a group of girls who suffered from a severe and contagious strain of boy fever, and as she had a predisposition for the affliction, she fell victim to it quite easily. I was a little more selective and therefore, once again, could not relate to my sister, and the chasm between us reappeared. Mom, as expected, enjoyed the tales of Penny's exploits but was marginally involved in my interests, which gradually returned to the realm of athletics and visits to the library. Masks can't stay on forever.

The day I was asked to join the volleyball team was one of the proudest and saddest moments of my youth. Mom was putting on makeup. She had a date. Again.

"What is it, Margaret?" My mother asked this question without the slightest disruption to her concentration as she outlined her lips in a deep shade of coral.

"I have a note for you from Coach Parker. He wants me to join the volleyball—"

"Can it wait, Margaret? I'm very late. PENELOPE! Did you take my blue eye shadow again?" She called out to my sister over my head and into the hallway outside the bathroom.

"I have to give him an answer tomorrow and you have to sign this—"

"Peggy, I said I don't have time now. Please get out of the way. I keep bumping into you." She made that face I hated, the one that made me feel like leftover dog food. Penny appeared with the eye shadow, and the two of them began a fifteen-minute conversation that included a debate about the shade of blue on her eyelids, another one about Penny's stupid fantasies of becoming a New York fashion designer, and ten more minutes on how high our mother should whip her hair.

"Mom, just tease your hair a little more at the top, like Marlo Thomas, but bigger."

"Marlo Thomas? I want it messy and sexy, like Raquel Welch, but wilder."

They sounded like Lucy and Ethel, but loonier.

Mother squealed with anticipation at the sound of an impatient car horn blowing outside. I watched as she collected all the paraphernalia and returned it to her makeup bag without another thought about my request. I blinked hard to keep the tears from coming, but the rage had balled up in my throat and I felt it rising. I was nauseated. I thought I would hurl. When she rushed past me and into the hallway, I spoke one word, and my voice was deep and unrecognizable. "Slut!"

She stopped with a start and turned to face me not quite believing her ears, or so it appeared from the look on her face. "What?"

I didn't know what to make of her steady gaze. *She's going to kill me*, I thought. No, that wasn't it. She was … punctured, deflated. Strangely, I felt no regret for saying it, but I wasn't stupid enough to repeat it. I held her gaze. She turned again and slowly walked to the door. She never forgave me.

Predictably, Penny married young and swiftly produced offspring, which swept away whatever lukewarm interest she had in continuing her education after high school. Our mother's delusions of Penny's New York adventures in the fashion world or marrying rich were never fulfilled.

She met Charles, the Virginian, as I like to call him, at a bar on the beach when he came to Miami for spring break right before taking the bar exam. Penny, now in her tender twenties and working as a receptionist for a chiropractor, refused to let go of her glory days in high school and spent most of her weekends foraging for men with her pathetic, over-made-up friends in every club in the city. Small-town Charles was dazzled and misguided by the seemingly sophisticated Penny, and they were married within the year. As soon as she spoke her "I do," she made the dutiful move to quaint Staunton, Virginia, where Charles Peterson, Esquire, and Mrs. Peterson began their mind-numbingly dull suburban life. The esquire spent long hours at his respectable yet unambitious little law office while Mrs. Esquire tended house, gossiped with other stymied housewives, and wiped spittle off baby chins.

I, however, plunged deep into academic coaching and have never come up for air. To outsiders, I seem devoted and possess a flawless work ethic. It's nothing but enmeshment. It's all I've ever had, and I cling to it like lint to wool.

Today, in our late middle age, my relationship with Penny is distant and complicated. I suffer from chronic envy of my twin sister. There are moments when regret eats at me for not accepting one of the promising romantic offers that came my way in younger days. Such relationships smelled of bondage, and after breaking free of my familial shackles, I couldn't see any contrast between what these lovely boys were offering and that which I had left behind. But on the rare occasions when I have been allowed to visit the dilapidated remnants of my family, fate steps in to redeem me as I watch my sister swim in an ocean of discontent and breathe the thick air that enfolds a meaningless and workaday life. Her conversation skills have been reduced to a whiny litany of complaints about her home, her husband, her kids, her grandkids. Marriage and family are wonderful, I'm sure, but in this garden variety, I want no part of it.

I suspect that, in some way, it is also the reason why Penny keeps me at arm's length. I suppose I represent missed opportunities and sacrificed freedom. I am a small window into a wide, bright, indomitable world, a window that she prefers to keep closed for fear she may want to jump.

But I miss Heather and Harry. One thing Penny and the Virginian deserve credit for is their children, now both young parents themselves. Maybe it was the small-town upbringing, or maybe deep-down Penny recognized the enormous dysfunction in which we grew up. Whatever the reason, she bore and raised two complete human beings, two siblings who seemed expatriates from another world, mutually respectful and fair, always looking out for each other's well-being in the most passionate way. My fantasy is that at some point in their lives, Penny had an epiphany of remorse, and told them about our own irreconcilable differences, and the two youths vowed not to forget so as not to repeat our history. Just daydreaming.

When we all get together at Penny's house for the odd holiday or significant life event, her home hints at warmth and joy. Harry's two children and Heather's one daughter coexist peacefully on the living room rug or in the backyard, the Virginian comes alive in his outpouring of hospitality, and my niece and nephew relish the opportunity to revisit the mischief of their childhood. Perhaps the whispered call of blood is louder than I think, because periodically I crave being in their midst, even if I must maneuver through the apathy with which my twin receives me.

"This summer's going to be crazy, Margaret." I hate her patronizing tone when she says my given name. "I can't see where there would be time for you to visit. It might be better to leave it for Christmas, darlin'." And I hate her fake and snobby Southern accent.

"What's going on?" Translation: What's your excuse now?

"Well, to begin with, Charlie's firm is involved in a case that has him traveling to North Carolina every couple of weeks. It's probably the biggest thing he's ever worked on." I hear disdain in those words. "Harry's working two jobs so he can take the kids to the mountains sometime before school starts up again, and Heather—

"Okay, okay, I get it. It's not a good time." It never is.

••

*J*ack takes a sip of his *café con leche* before speaking, and Grace writes notes in a small notebook while Mindy dictates something to her over the phone.

"Okay, this is what I've been able to put together so far," he begins. "I spoke to Sara Gerald, the VP of external affairs of the Alumni Association. She assured me that South Florida College is devoted to collaborating with the local community. It's simple. The center has always provided a place for our students to do their community service hours, so this is definitely a mutually productive partnership."

Grace finally hangs up her cell phone and I'm already halfway into my Cuban sandwich. I must say, I objected to going anywhere fancier than the university cafeteria for our quick lunch, but this sandwich is so good, I'm secretly happy my friend is such a spoiled brat. And Jack, saint that he is, wisely gives her anything she wants. Grace insisted that if we were going to take the time to leave the campus, we might as well head to Havana Harry's just a couple of blocks away, for a *real* lunch, not ham and cheese sloppily slapped between two sad-looking slices of bread, as she described it. After a bite of her chorizo empanada and a few groans of pleasure, she begins her debriefing.

"The scoop is that the struggling donors began to pull their support when the economy took a dive in 2008. They've been able to stretch their government dollars for the past twelve years, but now that's about to go away too. Most everyone left on the staff is there on a volunteer basis, and the place needs some serious repairs. I think whatever we're able to raise will have to go toward that first. You're there every week, Peggy. What do you think needs to be fixed first?"

"Probably air-conditioning and plumbing. The AC and heat are temperamental at best, and too many faucets leak."

"Okay, and next on the priority list should be the floors. Mindy said she saw more than one wheelchair get stuck on uneven or broken tiles."

Jack nods as he washes down a mouthful of his juicy roast pork with another sip of his *café*. I bet he's happy we came too.

"Well, prioritizing is good but let's wait and see how much money we'll have to work with." Jack's always the pragmatist. I've known these two for years, and I can say with conviction that I've never seen Jack make a decision or a statement that wasn't thoroughly considered. Grace is just too smart for her own good and can succumb to impulsivity at times, but she's adept at making hard turns to get back on track. And if individually they are forces to be reckoned with, as a team, they are awe-inspiring. I love them both. Having such solid people as friends is comforting.

When I first applied for a job in the athletics department at South Florida College, I had just turned forty-five years old. My midlife crisis manifested in an irrepressible desire to leave high school teaching after twenty years and a very well-established reputation, if I may say so, as a varsity coach. When the call came, I was faced with the daunting task of sitting in front of a hiring committee made up of eight members of the college's most senior faculty. My eyes skimmed across every countenance, each obligatory smile imbued with its own signature air—the scholarly, the pompous, the inconvenienced, the bored, and the self-righteous, all properly represented.

As I nervously surveyed the ill-concealed expressions, I noticed one face that stood out like a fresh, lone blade of grass surviving after a brush fire. The others whispered to each other for what seemed like an eon and pointed with arrogant superiority at different sections of my résumé, but this particular man squinted at them and then, almost apologetically, at me. He cleared his throat and took the lead, speaking first.

"I believe there is no question that Ms. Paulson has impeccable credentials, so perhaps we can begin with our questions without any further delay." His voice was measured and respectful, and although presiding over the proceedings was not his role, his initiative set the tone. I composed myself quickly, switched to professional mode, and ultimately got the job. I will forever be grateful to Jack for treating me like a colleague and not a criminal waiting for that condescending *hiring* squad to pull the trigger.

After that initial meeting, I didn't see much of Jack, as his activities in the music department didn't intersect much with mine in the athletics department. I met Grace entirely by chance, since we both worked at SFC but had never seen each other until Sylvia, our common denominator, introduced us at the annual college fund-raiser. A few months after that, she and Jack began a very covert romance, not for any question of propriety, as faculty couplings were not censured, but more because of a desire to guard the budding and still fragile relationship. Now, five years later, I revel in watching from a first-row seat as these two endearing middle-aged youngsters plan their wedding. It fills my heart and it fills the void.

The foodie group is also a respite from my loneliness. We just started our restaurant scavenger hunts a year ago, but what a difference it's made. I couldn't imagine my life without these women. Each, in a sharply distinctive way, stimulates a separate part of me. Sylvia's fierce passion for success challenges me to feel as fresh and new at what I do as the first day after graduation. Jo's authenticity inspires me to own and embrace who I am. Madeline teaches me every day what it is to be truly generous. Grace has a hypnotic effect on me when she speaks. Her words make everything profound and comprehensible. And little Mindy. I think that secretly, Mindy is everyone's role model although we old hens would never admit to it. She certainly personifies what I wish I had been when I was a younger woman: gifted with aplomb, quiet devotion, uncompromising loyalty. You can't *get* that way. It's inborn.

This new endeavor of ours with the community center brings with it some relief from the desolation that is my life right now. I can only imagine the Amazonian feats that we can accomplish together, and I am equal to the task, eager and hungry to belong.

My cell phone rings and Sylvia's neon name shines on the screen. "Hey Syl, I'm here with Jack and Grace going over some of the information we have on Oceanview. You're on speaker."

"Hey there," Grace and Jack chime in simultaneously.

"I'm kinda glad I got you all together because I have some news too," Sylvia announces. "I think we may be able to get the Napoleon Ballroom at the Deauville on the beach for our benefit."

"Holy cow, are you serious? That's where the Beatles played!" Grace says, choking a little on her Diet Coke.

"Yup! The publicity is worth solid gold to them, and since Jo is hooking us up with catering, it's not much of a hassle for them. But we have to decide soon on a date. I just threw in early September as a tentative. I thought it would be good for this to coincide with the beginning of the academic year since your alumni association is the principal sponsor."

"Geez, that's amazing! How do you pull these things off? Who do you know? Can we afford it?" Grace's excitement is making her cherub cheeks blush.

"Actually, they called me. They said they were contacted already by an influential SFC alumnus who seems very ardent about this project."

I know Sylvia. She's holding back something. Her voice has become slightly somber.

"Who is it, Syl?" I ask. Static. "Syl? Are you still there?"

A deep breath. "Richard Montiel."

Looks of astonishment dart around the table, and my eyes rest on my cell phone, as if Sylvia were materializing from it.

"Oh. My. God." Grace whispers the words deliberately and each one carries the weight of a million consequences as it is uttered.

I slump back into my chair and search desperately for a way to salvage this moment with some clever solution, but all I feel is paralyzing disgust with myself for having nothing to offer. "What are we going to do?"

"I don't know, Peggy. This is delicate. And it could get worse. He wants to meet with the organizers to talk about money. You and Grace are handling the money, Jack. It stands to reason that you two should be the ones to talk with him first." Sylvia seldom sounds this defeated.

"Oh *heeeell* no!" Grace's blushed cheeks have now turned ashen. "I won't be able to have a civil conversation with that man. What he did to Maddie was disgusting, and I know I'm going to say something if we're face to face."

In his silence, Jack looks at us with intent, as if waiting for us to give an obvious answer to a simple question. "Now wait a second. I understand that this is a little sticky, and that their divorce is unfortunate, but I think we need to keep the focus on what's important here. If we're going to do this, we have to do it right. We can't let personal agendas become obstacles. We'll have enough of those without creating them ourselves."

"Jack! I can't stand to look at that man and he knows it. When he finds out it's us, he'll quit being interested in the project in a nanosecond."

"He already knows, Grace," offers Sylvia's metallic voice.

Grace glares at the phone and her mouth opens slightly, but Sylvia is quicker. "The hotel invited the four of you to dinner so you could scope out the ballroom and talk to their marketing people."

I think Grace might cry from frenetic umbrage. She's having a tough time keeping her lips from quivering. "The four of us? What four?" The words are barely audible.

"You and Jack, and Rich and … Mercy."

"Mercy? His whore?"

It's too much for her. Grace explodes out of her chair, sliding it clear into the next table, and disappears to the restroom in a tidal wave of sound and fury.

So much for our Amazonian feats.

Madeline

I remember when Rich and I bought the chandelier that hangs over our majestic living room. In fact, I have vivid memories of every moment spent decorating our dream palace with the sweeping views of Biscayne Bay and the sparkly downtown Miami skyline. They made quite the background to our dinner parties on the massive Spanish Colonial dining room table with the splendid arrangement of always fresh flowers, surrounded by ten kingly chairs. How insignificant these things look now—the state-of-the-art entertainment equipment in the screening room; the romantic four-poster Alaskan king bed that holds the delicious secrets of our intimacy. I spent hours on that bed surrendering my body and my heart without reservation to this man I called my husband for nineteen years, a man I trusted implicitly, the father of my precious children, the man who betrayed me in the most heinous way.

Of all the corners in this fortress, the one place where I seem to be able to slow down the world when it spins out of control is the plush sapphire velvet couch in the blue room. The view of the bay outside helps me breathe when I feel choked by life. I wonder what he'll do with the boat. We hardly ever took it out. It's a sixty-foot decoration more than anything, purchased to impress. The rich warmth of the couch makes me feel consoled and protected.

My beagle Blaze and I are sitting here now trying to put all our ducks in a row, waiting for my friend, the attorney, to help me figure out in what brutal way I am to purge myself of everything that I have come to love and dismantle what I thought would always be my refuge. Blaze lifts her head from my lap, turns her face to one side, and says with no words, *Really? Girl, please, this is a no-brainer.* Then she closes her eyes and puts her head back on my lap. Blaze doesn't entertain drama. I guess her ducks are all neatly lined up. It's not that simple for me.

When I greet Mindy at the door, her eyes instinctively go to the soaring twenty-three-foot-high cathedral ceiling, and her mouth opens a bit in awe even though it's not the first time she's been here. I have seen that expression on the faces of many people when they walk in, and I can't help but smile bitterly.

Mindy Johnson is the youngest member of our roving foodie club and she is a breath of fresh air. She is a twenty-eight-year-old Jamaican powerhouse. A Harvard Law School graduate, she is deeply devoted to her mother and sisters, and is perhaps the wisest of us all even though we are significantly older. Sylvia met her at a party given by a Miami socialite whom Mindy had represented in a lengthy, turbulent divorce. She was instantly drawn to the young prodigy, and when we started the foodie club, Sylvia invited her despite the age difference. We wasted no time in falling in love with her. She was the perfect fit.

I kiss her and lead her into the den. "What can I get you to drink?"

"Diet Coke would be good, thanks."

She sits on a high bar chair at the massive marble island facing my gourmet kitchen while I get her a soda, then swiftly move to the bar to fix myself a Long Island iced tea. I detect a little worry in her eyes. "So what do you think? Any suggestions?"

"Is the decision to sell the house final?"

"It's not what I want, but Rich insists that's what we should do."

"What do *you* want to do?"

I look at her ready to answer and unexpectedly, a wave of despair washes over me. Instead of words, a despondent cry comes forth from my lips, and I dissolve into frantic sobs as I hide my face in the palms of my hands. Every worry and fear I've carried for months descend upon me all at once—the possibility of losing the house, my broken family, the pain in my kids' eyes on the morning their father moved out. When I emerge, Mindy sits quietly, barely breathing, looking at me with a mixture of compassion and discomfort. She's waiting for me to compose myself. Mindy is not one to dwell on emotions that are useless in solving pressing issues, and her pragmatism has a sobering effect.

"I'm so sorry about that. I'm a mess," I whimper as I walk to the nearest of eight bathrooms to search for a tissue.

"Really? You never look a mess. You always seem so together," she says with sincerity.

That makes me laugh. "It's just a front. Most of the time I don't know what I'm doing, but thanks, Mindy. Okay, so let's talk about this. I won't lie, I'm sick over having to give up my house and relocate my kids, but I'm being forced into it, so I want to figure out the best way to do this."

"When you say 'the best way,' what exactly do you mean?"

I'm a little puzzled by the question. "I want to get rid of all of this and see what we're left with," I say with a dismissive sweep of my hand that symbolically encompasses all the frills of my now defunct married life. "I want to renew my nursing license and go back to work."

"Not a chance." She takes out a pen and a legal pad.

"What do you mean? Why not? I have to do something, and all I've ever been is a nurse, although I haven't worked in twelve years."

Now she's writing feverishly on the legal pad without looking at me. Is she an attorney or a therapist? And what could she be writing? I'm not saying that much.

"I don't want you to even contemplate going back to work. At least not until the divorce is final. Look around you, Maddie. We're sitting in this multimillion-dollar mansion, you've been married for nineteen years, and you have two minor children.

That alone is enough to secure you a comfortable settlement at a minimum. Besides, Rich's international real estate business can take care of you well enough so you won't need a nurse's paycheck to supplement your income."

"Okay, but it's not just about the income. I need to do something other than ladies' lunches and spa days. I'm sick of it all."

"Fine. After the divorce is done, you can do whatever you want, but right now I want you to dismiss that notion from your mind. Trust me. I know what I'm doing. I suppose Richard's reasons for wanting to sell the house and its contents are financial?"

"Well, yes…" I hesitate. I guess that's the reason. "His business took a hard hit with the recession, and he said that even ten years later, the company's profits have never been the same. Before we separated, he mentioned several times that we would have to consider downsizing. I certainly can't pay for this house, and I assume he won't be able to either."

"You *assume*? It doesn't matter, there will be full financial disclosure on both parts when we begin divorce proceedings, and there is no prenup, so all bets are off."

I think I'm missing something here. "Wait, do you think there's a chance I won't have to leave my house?"

"I can't say right now, Maddie, but taking a hit doesn't mean he's bankrupt. You do know you are entitled to a settlement, right? And that could include the house if it's what you want and if it's at all possible. We'll see. If that's not feasible, we can think about an estate sale. I'm willing to bet you can get a significant sum. But there's lots of things we need to look at before we consider that. We do need to address child support. That's certain."

I'm overwhelmed. I hear bees buzzing in my ears, and their buzzing seems to be mixing with Mindy's voice. I don't want to do this. I want to turn the clock back to when I didn't know. I understand the cliché now. I *was* blissful in my ignorance.

••

*T*he jets shoot hot water from every angle of my luxurious shower. The burn feels good as it shrouds my body. The European stone is comforting under my feet. But I can't wash away the feeling that I sounded uninformed and out of touch with my own situation when I talked to Mindy. Maybe there are options I haven't considered because I'm so busy trying to avoid confrontation. All I want is peace. I don't want to fight. I just want all of this to go away. This is not how my life was supposed to be. When did it all go off the rails? I couldn't even begin to isolate the moment when it all turned left, but at some point, I felt it, and I decided to turn my face away from it. No need to deal with the unpleasant truth today when it might magically disappear tomorrow. Denial. Hello, my trusted friend.

When I began to date Richard Montiel in college, he appeared to be all that a well-brought-up girl should aspire to in a husband. Good churchgoing family, solid education, charming, attentive, wanted all the things I wanted out of life. No sign at all of what lurked within. Or was there, and I refused to see it?

Janet saw it. She warned me. On the day of our lavish wedding at Villa Vizcaya, I looked upon the elaborate European-styled gardens and the opulent Baroque room where

I stood as evidence of exclusive admission into a fairytale life, the granting of unspoken wishes. As she helped me dress, my high school friend cautioned me one last time. "You don't have to do this, Madeline. This guy is not for you."

I laughed it off. "You're so funny, Janet. I know you're kidding." And she watched me walk down that aisle into a golden life laced with control, and eventually betrayal. The wives of his friends and associates became my only friends. My only social activities were those sanctioned by him or his family. Little by little, I distanced myself from my own friends until there was virtually no contact. I allowed myself to be sucked into the Montiel bubble.

It wasn't all bad. The beginning was very good. When Rich made it big in real estate, the lifestyle was dazzling, especially for a girl from a humble middle-class family. When we traveled the world, the doors of every Ritz-Carlton would open to receive us; we had a table reserved in perpetuity at Le Bernardin in New York City, where we often entertained shiny, glamorous people. We both drove the latest Mercedes-Benz custom models, Rich's everyday wardrobe was almost always Armani, and as for me, suffice it to say I had a front seat at every fashion show from New York to Milan. Yes, the beginning was very good. Then came our perfect children. If life was good before David and Iris, when they arrived, I thought I held the world in my hand.

At the peak of this life bathed in pixie dust, we built our palatial home. One of three that became the Montiel compound. His parents on the left, his sister on the right. It made sense since they were all partners in Montiel International. I confess, I liked their energy, their passion for adventure and good living.

And then there was the sex. The lifestyle was the pull, but our sex life was the opium. The demon knew how to strip me of inhibitions, and I surrendered to mind-blowing sensations. His warm breath as he whispered in my ear, the taste of his mouth, our smells mixing into an erotic and familiar scent, his skin glistening with perspiration, the electric feel of his touch, the thundering beat of his heart on my chest, the seductive rhythm of our bodies in unison. Every encounter was an adventure. That never changed. Not even, I'm ashamed to admit, on the night after I found him with his whore on our bed—the first of three times I found him with her. Just hours later, on that same bed, I made a pointless and wretched attempt to mark my territory with frantic, raging lovemaking.

That uncomfortable yet familiar chill ran through me once again on that fateful evening when Rich said he would be meeting with his partner, and not to wait up for him. And even with my warning system flashing bright red, I told him

I'd take Iris to a movie and David to his friend's house. I pretty much just served him the opportunity on fine china.

It was another clue in a pattern of inconsistencies. At first, I brushed off the signs. The cell phone shut off during peak business hours, the many Little League games missed on Saturdays, the late nights at work, even the diminished desire for intimacy—all this I dismissed easily.

The turning point came when Rich canceled a family vacation we had been planning for months. Just a week before our Disney cruise, when David and Iris were wild with anticipation, he said he couldn't leave because of some big closing on a land acquisition that required his and only his presence. This late in the game, it would crush the kids, so he benevolently suggested that we go without him, that perhaps I should take my sister or a friend in his place. He would pay for any transference fees. The saint. His timing and execution were brilliant. This one I couldn't overlook. And so began the journey that would lead me to the grisly moment of discovery.

"Now David, promise me you'll keep an eye on that cell phone in case I call you," I said as he unbuckled his seatbelt.

"Yes, Mom."

I feel like shaking him every time he gives me the preteen eye roll, which is a lot.

"I'll pick you up before eleven o'clock, okay? No argument."

Then he gave me a condescending look like only a twelve-year-old could.

"Again, yes, Mom. So where are you off to?" An obnoxious preteen, but still my gallant son.

"I'm going to pick up your sister from her art class and take her to the movies. Your dad's working late at the Giordanos'."

"The Giordanos? Are you sure? The Giordanos are in Washington. Emily wasn't in school the whole week."

I thought the lump in my throat was my heart, and I feared I would vomit.

"Really?" I tried to even out my voice. "I must be confused. He said he had to review some contracts with either Lou or Mike. It must be Mike, then. Okay, honey, have fun." Now I couldn't wait to get rid of my baby boy.

"Remember, be ready before eleven," I yelled as he sprinted to his friend's front door. He turned and put his hand up. I couldn't tell if he was saying "bye" or "stop". It didn't matter. There was something pressing harder on my mind. I drove a few yards away and stopped the car. I dialed Rich's cell. Voicemail. I dialed his office. That was stupid. It was seven o'clock in the evening and there was no one there. And even if he had been there, he wouldn't have answered. Iris's class would not be over for another half hour. I had plenty of time. But I didn't want to do it. What if it was what I thought it was? Did I want to know? I had to know, once and for all.

I turned the ignition and allowed the car to coast, not entirely decisive as to what direction to take. But the car seemed to know, and a few minutes later, I stopped two houses from hers. The street was quiet. Farther down from her house, I could make out two boys on skateboards, the only people visible. Her garage door was open, and there were no cars in it or in her driveway, but I could see shadows behind the curtains over the front window. Her kids and her mother were home. I didn't realize my chest had been resting on the steering wheel until I allowed myself to lean back and exhale. He wasn't there. I turned the ignition again and as I drove to pick up Iris from the art studio, my breathing stabilized.

"Hi, Mommy!" Iris always dives into the back seat of the car as if it were a swimming pool.

"Hi, baby, how was it?"

"It was cool! We're doing pottery. It's kinda gross at first, but it's fun. I'm making you a flowerpot. It gets really messy and you have to keep up with the wheel. I can't do it by myself yet, so Rae has to help me." And so my nine-year-old ADD child begins a new stream-of-consciousness account of her latest art project. "Are we going to the movies?"

"Yes, baby, but maybe we should stop by the house so you can clean up."

"I'm not that dirty, Mommy!"

"You have clay stains on your shirt, Iris. It's just going to take a minute."

I think she sensed my tension because she was too quick to give in. Would I regret the sudden detour? As I turned into our street, she was listing all the colors available for painting after the projects were finished.

"… and there's this really pretty yellow that I think would be nice if you put the pot in the backyard."

I now had a panoramic view of our three-house compound on the right with the tall, concealing hedges that surround each house, and the bay on the left.

"… but if you want it for the front porch, I think a rust color would be best. Rust is like a brick color, Mommy."

Rich's car is in our driveway … and so is hers. I shouldn't have told him the house would be empty until late. The nerve! Not that it would've made matters better if I hadn't told him. They would've gone somewhere else. It would've just delayed the inevitable. In one last ditch effort at holding on to hope, I thought maybe I was jumping to conclusions without hard evidence.

"So what color do you want, Mommy? Look! Daddy's home."

I stopped the car, but I didn't have much time to think of a way to keep Iris from running off to see her precious daddy. I parked in my in-laws' driveway. I wondered if Marie and Richard Sr.

knew she was here. They wouldn't think anything of it, anyway. She'd been working in their company for some time. She'd even been to our homes for business and social events many times. Our children played together often. And even if they suspected their golden son of anything inappropriate, wouldn't they just sweep it under the rug? Isn't that what Marie had done for years in her own marriage?

"Honey, I gotta talk to Daddy for a few minutes. Why don't you go see what Grandma's got cookin'? I'll call you so you can come take a bath in a little bit." I thought that might keep her away for a while.

"A bath? We don't have time for that! Ask Daddy if he wants to come to the movies with us."

I opened my own door and walked in as quietly as a thief. I was still praying that I would find them sitting in my den looking at paperwork like they'd done so many times before, but what were the odds of that, really? The den was empty and dark. Not a creature was stirring … I looked up the grand staircase with its intricate iron grillwork and into the marble landing. That too was eerily quiet and dark. I wanted to climb the stairs, but I couldn't move. Two cars in the driveway, and silence in the house. I knew what I would find upstairs. I couldn't wallow in hunches and suppositions any longer. I walked up stealthily. I reached the door to my own bedroom.

It was ajar. The arrogance! How entitled does a man have to feel to dare bring his mistress into his marriage bed?

With one gentle push from my finger, my nightmare came to life, more vicious, more disturbing, more sickening than my suspicious mind could ever make it. Their eyes met mine and unexpectedly, a kind of warped peace came over me, because now I knew, and the uncertainty was finally over. Or so I thought.

●●●

I've lost track of time with this stroll down Ugly Memory Lane, and the tips of my fingers are pruny. As I reach for the knob to turn off the shower, a horrifying, deafening, shrill sound makes me cover my ears instinctively. And then I realize *I'm* screaming. Loud enough to bust a lung, but not loud enough to kill the sound of my world imploding into nothingness.

I have good days and bad days. Today has been a doozy of a bad one.

"Mommy, are you sleeping?"

I hear Iris's soft voice very near me. I open my eyes even though my eyelids have become red, heavy shades from incessant crying for God knows how long before I went unconscious.

"Mommy, are you sick?"

My stomach constricts at the look of worry in my baby girl's eyes. I push the sack of despair that is my body into a sitting position.

"No, my love, just taking a little nap. Where did Daddy take you today?" I sit her soft, fleshy body on my lap and stroke her long coffee brown hair. She looks so much like her father; shared features that trigger such different emotions in me. One face gives me life, the other twists my insides with resentment.

"We had lunch at the beach and then went to Boomers. We rode the go-karts and played miniature golf. I beat David!"

"Oh, he must've been thrilled about that."

"He was so mad!" She laughs heartily. It does my soul good. "Daddy says he needs to talk to you."

I'd rather jump into a piranha-infested swamp than talk to *him* today.

"Okay, baby, I'll call him later. I gotta see about dinner right now."

"No, I mean now. He's downstairs."

I stop cold on my belabored walk toward the bathroom. *Why, God?* I don't think I can take much more today.

"Tell him I'll be down in a minute."

"You're not gonna be mad, right?" Iris asks anxiously. My poor child. What are we doing to her?

"No, baby, of course not. Nothing to be mad about. Go on, I'll be right down." I will say this for Rich, he has been very careful to keep our discussions and arguments away from the kids, but it's impossible for them not to be caught in our dark energy in some way.

He's sitting in the den with David, and apparently, I have interrupted a very intense conversation because my son looks at me wide-eyed and proceeds to leave the room without even a hello to me or a good-bye to his father. David and Rich have always had a volatile relationship.

"Hi, Madeline, how are you? His round face looks tanned, and I notice he's let his hair grow a little. He's slimmer too. That woman is important to him, no question about that. But he's still short.

I sit next to him, and I wonder if he can see the death mask under my hastily applied makeup. "I'm good. Looks like the kids had a good time today. Thanks for taking them."

"No need to thank me. I love them, you know? I like spending time with them." *Really? You never took them anywhere by yourself when we were together.* "Yeah, I must say, you have been very good about that."

"That's what I wanted to talk about. Listen, Maddie, I know you've started on the divorce and I do think it's best. I want you to know that I will do everything I can to make this as smooth and painless as possible for everyone. I want us to do all we can for our kids. Let's stay friends … for them."

What a prince. "Thanks, Rich. They are my biggest concern. They're both at tough ages to be dealing with this. I don't want them to feel shortchanged by either one of us."

"Right. Exactly. That's why I wanted to be honest with you, you know? Completely upfront."

Something's coming. Now what? I shift in my seat to prepare myself.

"Umm, you see … Mercy and I are … seeing each other, you know. Uh … we're dating, I guess."

So there it is. The whore! My mouth feels like I sucked on a tube of Krazy Glue. Up to now it hadn't occurred to me that they were that serious. I guess it makes sense. He trashed our entire life together for her.

"Look, it—it … just happened. After I asked you so many times to forgive me and you refused, I just didn't know what to do. She was there and, well, we understand each other."

So, what I'm hearing is that it's my fault that he accidentally tumbled into her vile, filthy privates—*over and over*—because I refuse to live the rest of my life with a manipulative, cheating dirtbag. I want to kill them both!

"Does your family know?" It's all I'm able to say, but of course they know.

"Yes, they're uncomfortable about it, but they don't really meddle."

You mean they enable you, you degenerate moron.

"And, well, the kids know too. We were with her today. I should've told you, but it wasn't planned, and I promise you that I will tell you in the future."

"I see." Now I understand why Iris thought I would be upset. This is unqualified humiliation. *I'm going to make you pay, Richard Montiel.* I rise from the couch and look down at his face. I think he's holding his breath. He's a little afraid. Good. "It's not my business anymore. Are the kids okay with it?"

"David isn't. He wants nothing to do with Mercy." *My beautiful boy.* "Iris seems okay."

"Fine. I wish you the best, Rich." I walk to the kitchen and he realizes it's his cue to leave. As soon as he closes the door behind him, I reach for the phone. All at once, the situation is bathed with clarity. I still feel the sting in my wounds, but I no longer feel afraid to move forward.

"Mindy, we need to talk. I've made some decisions … Yes … I want it all."

Sylvia

I think I'm getting a migraine. How could they do this? Do they really think this is a good thing? What message am I sending that could prompt these women to put me through this? I'm not doing it! "MINERVAAAAAA!"

"Yes, Sylvia?" She answers even before the door is fully open. Less than three seconds. That's a well-trained assistant, although using her given name is always effective.

"Close the blinds. Do you have my migraine pills?" My elbows are firmly planted on my desk, and I do not dare open my eyes or stop pressing my fingers to my temples for fear my brains will ooze out of my ears.

"Syl, are you sure you want to take those?" I can sense the hesitation in her voice, and I understand and appreciate her concern. After all, those pills could mellow an angry bull, but this is not a good time to question me. I open my eyes to slits with superhuman effort.

"Minnie, if I'm asking it's because I need them." My words drip in controlled aggravation. I see a flash of gray skirt disappear through the door even as the blinds complete their graceful descent from ceiling to floor, and a cool muted dusk envelops my office. The white lacquer credenza slowly loses its gloss and seems to join me on my way to slumber.

I feel some remorse about dumping my distress on Minnie when I truly believe my beloved friends (and I use "beloved" with the most cynical of intents right now) are the reason for this incapacitating headache.

A perfectly good lunch ruined by this ridiculous obsession with getting me a man. My friends are all a bunch of pimps, that's what they are. I don't want a man, I certainly don't need a man, not to mention that I have no time for a man. I thought it was strange that they all had the time for a random lunch in the middle of the week. I should've listened to my gut.

"Here you go, Syl." Minnie returns with a glass of water and two horse-tranquilizer-sized pills. She's right. I need to go easy on these, but if I don't take them right now, the rest of my day will be as pointless as that lunch with The Pimpettes.

"Hold my calls for about an hour." As Minnie closes the door ever so gently, the warm plush couch embraces me, and I feel my indignation subsiding. I know they mean well, and I realize that I'm probably angrier with myself than I am with them. Why am I unable to conceal whatever repressed fantasy I have about being with someone?

But singles mingling events? Where was the idea born that I would love an evening spent with men from a matchmaking service as a fiftieth birthday gift? No, it's ludicrous. It smells of desperation. Maybe they do see right through me. Especially that Grace. Sometimes she looks at me and I think she's drilling right through my eyeballs and into my soul. Don't ever assume you're fooling Grace. I swear she's a witch.

Oh, heavens. I have to admit—there are those times, if I allow myself to stop the merry-go-round that is my life for just a second, when I do wish I had a relationship with a nice, solid, genuine, no-game-playing guy like Grace has. Don't we all want that, if we're truly honest?

But getting over Roger took me to the brink of insanity, and I do not wish to even remotely revisit that place. I even wonder sometimes if I'll ever be over it.

The migraine has lost its edge and I feel a silky daze sweeping over me. I'll keep my eyes closed just for a little while …

I'm looking up at something as I shield my eyes from the sun. I hear loud swear words coming from above. It's the roof of my old house in the suburbs of Orlando, and Roger is doing the swearing. I look around anxiously to see if anyone is listening. Is this a dream? It looks very familiar. Now he's slamming tools. I can't take it anymore. Magically, I appear next to him on the roof and I've taken over the task of replacing the broken shingles. Roger watches with his signature sneer for a few seconds and suddenly, he is no longer in the scene. I look around again, this time searching for him. A wave of misery and loneliness washes over me, but I continue working. The sound of the hammering is earsplitting at first. I feel the pounding in my head. Now it's beginning to abate as it mixes with soft whimpering. Someone's touching my shoulder and saying my name. Did he come back to help me? But it's not his voice.

"Sylvia? Syl? Sylvia, wake up."

I struggle to open my lead-heavy eyelids. Minnie is tenderly holding my shoulders. "You were crying in your sleep. Are you okay?"

I slowly sit up as I try to shake the fuzz from my head. And then, without a word, I lay my forehead on Minnie's shoulder, and she gets it. She embraces me softly and remains quiet until I'm able to gather myself.

I don't know what I would do without Minnie, although I would never tell her. It scares me to think how well she reads me and how much she knows about me that no one else at the magazine knows. She's the quintessential all-business assistant, but in moments like this, she feels more like a younger, but more emotionally mature sister.

"How long have I been out?" My mouth feels cottony.

"About forty-five minutes, but you've been sobbing for about ten. I'm sorry I woke you, but I was starting to worry. You know I don't like when you take those pills."

"Okay, I'm fine. Give me a few minutes to clear my mind and fix my makeup, and we'll get to work. Anything I have to take care of right away?"

"Not right now. You have a meeting to finalize the layout for the issue on honeymoon locations but that's not until three thirty. Your friend Madeline called, though. She said to call her if you have a chance."

Not exactly thrilled to speak to any of these girls right now, but Maddie never calls me at work. "Thanks, I'll call her. Tell the team I also want to discuss the October and November issues. I want to kill the white after Labor Day article and look at the proofs for the shoot on the best fall foliage cities." Nothing clears my foggy brain better than work. "And Minnie, I'll need a fifteen-minute walk-by."

Minnie nods, knowing exactly what I mean.

I dial Maddie on my way to the bathroom. "Hi Maddie, what's up?"

"Hey, Syl, I just wanted to check up on you 'cause I thought you looked a little peeved when we told you about your birthday gift. Were you mad?" I glare down at the cell phone sitting on the sink top as I reapply some blush to my tired cheeks.

"Well, no, I wasn't mad exactly, I was just surprised. I'm still kinda' confused as to whether it's a gag or it's for real."

She laughs brightly through the speaker. "No, it's for real.

We thought you'd get a kick out of it. You *are* mad!"

Not mad anymore, but I'm certainly getting irritated now. "No, it's fine. I appreciate it, I just don't know if I'll ever have the time to use it."

"Oh Sylvia, look, I'm sorry if we offended you. That certainly wasn't our intention."

I know that.

"But listen, my friend, if you don't want to do it, you're not obligated. We can return it and get you something else."

"We'll talk about it later, Maddie. I gotta get ready for a meeting."

Immediately after we hang up, I wonder: Why didn't I instantly accept her offer to exchange the event voucher for something else? Was it out of politeness, or does the adventuresome part of me want to try it out? What's happened to that part of me? Before the magazine took off, I would've found it funny, exciting, and I would've had a *why not?* attitude about it. Now it just feels like an interruption from my well-oiled routine, a deviation from my comfort zone. Oh my, I have a comfort zone. When did I decide I needed a safe place?

Come on, sweets, you know exactly when it happened.

Yes, I do know.

I'll tell you what," he said. "You come down to the court after class, we'll shoot some hoops. The first one to make twenty, wins. If I win, you go out with me."

"What if I win?" I said.

"If you win, you pick the restaurant."

Well played. How could I resist? Roger was scary in a charismatic way. I'm a fixer. I like to repair broken things, situations, people. Not long after I graduated college, I went bounding into my marriage to Roger, as I do with everything I undertake in life, secure in the knowledge that it would be a success, free of negativism, and confident that I could do all and be all. I alone held the key to our world, I had a bird's-eye view of it, and I would give meaning to it. Sure, Roger had some emotional issues stemming from childhood disappointments, but I had enough love to make up for his family's lack. He was emotionally stunted, self-absorbed, calculating, crass, even bordering on violent at times. My love would heal him. It wasn't a marriage. It was a thirty-year project.

Some called it innocence, some called it optimism, some even called it devotion. Every time I look in the mirror, I'm forced to face the fact that it was delusion.

Confession: Self-reliance, being in command of my surroundings, and winning at all costs is my sole purpose of existence. The heartbreaking fact is that I have paid a price so high that I can barely stand to admit it. Sylvia the Woman is in here somewhere but tragically lost. In her place, Sylvia the Conqueror has taken over, which I have learned is the biggest turnoff to any male of the species, who understandably will run from the perceived threat of emotional castration.

In hindsight, the question I should've asked myself in those early years was, What do you want more, Sylvia, to have the perception of control, to "fix" all that is broken in your quest for a world close to perfect, or to allow your man to be a man, to let go and trust him once or twice to find his own path to healing? But I had no self-awareness then. Not sure I have much now where men are concerned.

The old platitude about a man's ego being fragile shouldn't be dismissed as triviality. It is a fatal mistake to take that premise for granted. I designed our life together. I set up everything that turned out well and stepped in to repair what didn't. Roger had no role, and the emasculation made him lazy. So, one day, I don't know when, my marriage died, and a third party made her entrance. There's always some obliging female waiting in the wings to pick up the pieces of a broken man and worship him back to life.

Our love wasn't based on respect and affection, the cornerstones of the magnificent mutuality that love should be. Instead, the to-and-fro of our dissonant dance left me with a mixture of feelings — the resignation of an animal in captivity tossed together with the sexual intoxication of our youth that gave Roger a manipulative edge.

The long distance didn't help either. Roger insisted that the navy building contract in the Bahamas was an inconvenient but small sacrifice to make in exchange for the money we would be getting. Some things are *really* more important than money.

With little to do but drink incessantly during downtime while building the new hospital, surrounded by the predominantly female staff stationed in the temporary island clinic, Roger discovered that restlessness and temptation made for a deadly cocktail.

The call could not have come at a worse time. The house was full of Jasmine's friends, all a-giggle over my eight-month-pregnant daughter and the sea of baby accoutrements that bathed her. I rushed to answer and finally silence the unrelenting ring of the kitchen phone. I remember seeing Josh come in through the front door to begin loading his very manly truck with his young wife's treasures, all wrapped in butter-yellow ducks, caramel bears, and mint-green frogs, and topped with oversized bows in more sickly-sweet pastels.

"Syl?" The loud background noise was jarring. "Sylvia, can you hear me?" His words were slurred. It wasn't the first time he had called while buzzed, but never while still at whatever drinking dive he was patronizing that evening.

"Speak up, Rog, it's so loud."

"I don't know what … do … Syl."

"What? I didn't hear that, Roger."

Josh popped his head in the kitchen door.

"I'm not … appy, and … don't know … to do." Was he crying?

"Roger, you're scaring me, what's going on? Are you safe? Just come home." Silence and then a dial tone. Disconnected.

"What's up?" Josh was still at the door.

"I'm not sure. Something's wrong over there."

Josh dialed Roger's cell phone at least four times but the calls went straight to voicemail. Each time I saw him redial, my heart rate doubled. I didn't know what was going on, but suddenly I felt myself start to hyperventilate. On the other side of the kitchen, or what seemed to me far in the distance, I heard Josh speaking unintelligible words that started and stopped in random intermittence. I rubbed my tear-streaked face with the back of my hand. Why did I feel like something was about to take my whole world from my hands and rip it into confetti? Who was Josh talking to? Jasmine's and some other girl's disembodied faces blocked my view.

"PICK UP THE DAMN PHONE AND TALK TO YOUR DAMN WIFE, YOU BASTARD!" I heard that clearly. Was he talking to Rog? Was my husband all right? I looked at my daughter's face and it seemed distorted, as if I were looking out of a fishbowl.

"Damn coward!" Josh whispered under his breath, but somehow, I read his lips. "Sylvia, go upstairs. I'll come up and talk to you in a bit. Jas, go with her. The ladies and I will finish cleaning up here."

I didn't have any idea what was going on, but oddly, I complied with Josh's request without question. I didn't know what he knew, but whatever it was, it was so earth-shattering that it had to be delivered cautiously. As I walked toward the stairs, I heard him murmur to Jasmine and I slowed down my ascent. I turned to the mirror hanging on the wall and was horrified at the abstract mess made by tear-smudged makeup that looked back at me. I tried to ignore it and concentrate on Josh's muted voice, but all I was able to hear was "not coming back."

It was enough.

•••

*R*oger did come back eventually, but only to meet with lawyers and sign the divorce papers. He moved in with Hope, a navy nurse stationed on the island, and I was left in isolation with the unfading scar of my husband's betrayal. When you scorn someone you love, the bond somehow disintegrates. Pedestals crumble to the touch, and all you're left with is dusty hands.

Lost in endless periods of contemplation, I replayed every moment of the whirlwind that began with that phone call. My world didn't stop spinning until I received the final divorce decree. In the thick of my moroseness, I could not defeat reality, battle as I tried. Until one day, during a rain-soaked run, the realization that I no longer grieved for Roger but for Sylvia brought me to an abrupt stop. I felt worn out, but not physically. I was tired of feeling sorry for myself. Standing there, sopping wet, I owned the colossal mistake of trying to make my marriage a one-woman show, and my neglect in seeing the repercussions. I cut my losses, blinked the rain from my eyes, and refocused. At that moment, something changed. Everything changed.

I crossed a threshold on that day, and when I did, a brand-new life began. I sold our house, which Roger's guilt generously granted without caveats, and splurged on my ocean-view condo in South Beach. Doors began to open, and my horizon expanded—a promotion at the Herald, a hefty raise, more freelance work than I could handle, and a renewed fire to start my own magazine. I saved every penny I could and called on favors owed by powerfully connected publishers, editors, and fellow photographers.

And I have friends now. Good ones. Well, we all have our issues with the world and with each other, but we always come back to center because we have an unspoken understanding of the significance of female support. I've known some of them longer than others, and yet I find that the unifying element is that the school of hard knocks has taught every one of us that no male is equipped to fulfill every emotional and complex female need. Empowering knowledge.

Only six years after my rebirth, my world is unrecognizable. Yes, sacrifices have been necessary. I've had to stifle the longing for romantic partnership, but it's a reasonable price to pay for sovereignty over my life. I will never go back to who I was, and I'll be damned if I ever let any man take me back to the dark side.

I arrive at the conference room still hungover from the effect of the pills, trying hard to sound sharp. If I can submerge myself in the meeting and get in my decision-making zone, I'll snap out of it faster. I give the agenda a focused glance to convey to everyone sitting at the long table the impression that I have my wits about me.

"I don't want to spend a long time on this today. I want to finalize the current issue, make sure we're good with page count, and if anyone has some ideas for October and November, I'll listen."

A wave of throat-clearing, bodies straightening in chairs, and papers rustling follows. I'm back in control. "Jane?"

"The favorite lingerie survey, we thought it would be interesting to ask men too, instead of just women."

"Nobody cares what men think about lingerie, really. Women are going to buy what they like, and men just want it off. Next." It doesn't escape me that the two male editors present exchange meaningful looks.

"We have a good selection of fall recipes from which you can choose, Sylvia."

"What's the theme?"

"Uh … well, fall."

"Fall recipes in the October issue. I think it's been done, don't you? Where's the original twist?"

"Healthy foods for football gatherings?"

"Autumn harvest ingredients?"

"Cozy one-pot meals?"

The ideas begin to overlap as they flow through the room. They all sound stale to me. I won't waste any more time on it. "I want to choose four or five recipes by the end of this week. I'll let you figure it out." I say this to no one in particular. "I would also like to see drafts for reviews on at least three possible Academy Award contenders for the upcoming season no later than Monday. Let Martinez know."

"Sylvia, Martinez comes back from vacation on Friday. He won't have time."

The effort to look and sound alert is exhausting. I'm done. I try to oxygenate my brain with a deep intake of air, which I'm sure looks like exasperation. "Okay, we have two choices, then. He works through the weekend, or we outsource to an independent critic. I know a few people we can call. Let me know what you decide."

As instructed, Minnie appears on the other side of the glass wall making gestures that indicate she has something so important for me to address, that the meeting must be interrupted. This was one of her first lessons when she became my assistant. Always come and check on me fifteen minutes after a meeting starts. If I need to bail because of boredom, indisposition, or repressed frustration, pretend I have a call or an issue that must be handled right away. If it's going well, a gentle nod will let you know to keep walking. It's a good way to remove myself elegantly.

The stack of messages on my desk when I return from the meeting is short. Thank God because I think I may go home at a decent time today. That whole singles event thing triggered a wave of sentimentality I didn't think I could emerge from, and my energy is sapped. Six messages—two from the Deauville (I wonder what Grace and Jack have decided to do about that sticky dinner. Fragile situation); two from Tony Clifton (who's that? Oh yeah, the reporter from that New York TV station. I still don't know why they want to do a feature on me); one from Grace's friend Fanny (oh geez, Grace's shower! Gotta get moving on that); one from Synergy: "Please call to select your event and confirm a date" (oh crap! It's that dating thing. Are you freakin' kidding me?). I bet Minnie chuckled while taking that message. I'll call Fanny. It's all I can handle right now.

Even before I pick up the receiver, the intercom beeps. "Syl, Tony Clifton is on line two. Third time today. He's been a real pain in the posterior, that one. Could you *pleeease* talk to him?" Minnie's plea sounds genuinely desperate.

"Okay, I got it." I press button number two. "Sylvia Sabatino."

"WHOA! No way! I finally got you on the phone?" A little too friendly for a first contact, I think.

"What can I do for you, Mr. Clifton?"

"Mr. Clifton? Ugh! That sounds awful. How 'bout you call me Tony, and I'll call you Sylvia?"

Really? This is how you get an interview from someone you've never met? Bizarre. Breathe, Sabatino. "Nooo, I don't think so," I manage to say with my most patient of tones. "How about you call me Ms. Sabatino and I call you Mr. Clifton to start with, and we see how it goes, okay?" I think I crossed the line between patient and patronizing, but I don't care.

"All right then, as you wish," he says after a brief silence. "Ms. Sabatino, WCNY is doing a ten-profile series on successful women in business, media, and the arts. We'd like you to be one of the ten. No, no … we would be *honored* if you would be one of the ten." The way he said the word "honored" makes me want to shoot up insulin. This guy's a disrespectful buttwipe! I notice my right foot has begun an involuntary tapping to the beat of my shallow breathing.

"Now listen here, Mr. Sarcasmo, you must have a self-destructive streak in you. The way I see it, you want something from me, not the other way around. Your demeanor is unprofessional, so you have two options: If you want me to even consider cooperating on this interview, check yourself, or kindly stop calling my office and find some other successful woman to take your twaddle. Is that clear?"

More silence. "Crystal. Evidently, my approach on this initial phone call is all wrong and I do apologize, Ms. Sabatino. Please chalk it up to excessive exuberance over finally speaking to you. I propose that we do this some other time and start over.

Again, please forgive my lack of professionalism." The voice on the line is an octave lower. Is this the same man?

"Uhm… okay, that's probably a good idea." What did I just say? I'm totally off-balance right now. I didn't expect him to give up the swagger that easy. Was I too harsh?

"I'll call you again sometime later this week. You have a good day … *Sylvia*." *Click*. He hung up. He actually hung up on me! He's gotta be mentally ill. Or a douche with a capital *D*.

Josephine

*T*he kitchen at the boutique hotel where I spend my working days is my happy place. It's my respite from the mundane. I t ' s my dwelling of choice. It's where I nurture my calling and achieve Zen. Watching my team lovingly work on whatever creations we have concocted for the dessert menu is nothing short of paradise. As I take my ritual walk around the prep tables in a drift of contentment, I peer over their shoulders at gentle fingers delicately manipulating a fondant embellishment or melting a silky chocolate ganache, and I know deep inside, this is where I'm meant to be.

My culinary education was comprehensive enough that I can cook anything but being a pastry chef is what comes easily to my nature. And the one aspect of my profession to which I surrender with most delight is teaching the young cooks who come into my kingdom. In those moments when I find myself sharing what I know with an eager and promising new chef, I offer myself unconditionally to the task and find tranquility and balance. But now more pressing business is at hand.

"Okay everybody, gather round. Let's talk about this fund-raising dinner." I sit on a metal stool as they all surround the table and I spread several versions of a five-course menu. "I've got good news and bad news." Some take deep breaths, others lock eyes with each other. "The good news is that I think I finally figured out a viable menu. The bad news is that we're going to do most of it ourselves." A few grunts, but the reaction is not as bad as I expected.

"I thought you said Chef Mancuso upstairs was all for giving us a hand." Carmen, the newest member of our team and the least experienced, voices what other more seasoned members are afraid to say. Chef Mancuso is the magnificent executive chef in the hotel restaurant, and we were counting on him to take over the logistics of this project considering that down here in our kitchen, the focus is just desserts.

"We'll have some help from his team, but I've decided I want to oversee this job myself." A subtle cloud of dissension glides through the room. It's understandable. I suddenly feel the need to challenge myself, and I'm asking them to sink or swim right along with me. "Come on guys, this is a fantastic opportunity for all of us. Everyone here has been to culinary school and we can cook anything. Yes, I get that most of us have been doing pastry for a while, but if you weren't here, chances are you'd be cooking savory somewhere else." My feeble attempt at a pep talk is interrupted by the ringing of the kitchen phone.

"Jo, it's the front desk. Sylvia is here to see you?" My assistant, Chef Bruno, holds out the receiver for me.

"Oh? Okay, tell them to send her down. Carmen, could you fix us two lattes, please?"

After the obligatory introductions, kisses, and hellos, Sylvia and I settle in my sanctum, my old pantry turned office. Sylvia and I have been friends since I catered her magazine launch party, and I can say with certainty that she's only come to the hotel a handful of times even after repeated invitations. I'm drawn to her energy and her passion for anything she undertakes, but if I were to pinpoint a fault line in our friendship, I would have to say that I'm bothered by how everyone around her must dance to the beat of her drum to be in her life. Most of the time, I attribute it to her impossible schedule, but sometimes I feel a twinge of discomfort from always having to be the flexible one. It's not congruent with my personality, but it's become an unspoken agreement between our group of friends that Sylvia is the natural leader, and I've just gone along with it.

"So to what do I owe the honor, Miss Busy Bee? The only way I can get you over here is when I lure you with food, which by the way if you want lunch, they're making a killer chicken and creamy curry wrap upstairs."

Sylvia sighs with regret. "No honey, I have to meet this mutant TV reporter from New York for an interview I've been putting off too long. I tell you what though, I'd much rather hang here than eat with that sleaze."

"Okay then, so we're having crabby mood on lettuce and tomato for lunch today. Got it. Now, the fund-raiser: I can tell you that we probably won't have to worry about food as an expense. I have two restaurants and three major supermarkets that want to donate food in exchange for a sponsorship mention, but I need some numbers. I have enough kitchen staff for almost anything, but I can't rustle up servers if I don't know how many we need."

Carmen appears with two oversized white cups of steaming, frothy coffee and sets them on my desk.

"Nothing's set in stone yet, but I can tell you that more than two hundred tickets have been sold so far, and we're not even close to the date."

A small lump forms in my throat, and Carmen's naturally protruding eyes grow to the size of eggs. She gives me a look that screams "panic!" and withdraws to the kitchen. "Wow! Do we have a cap?"

"Not really, but if that number doubles, we'll have to hire a professional to help us. None of us have the time or the know-how to manage something that big. Which brings me to the real reason I'm here. When I called Fanny Newhart to discuss Grace's shower, I mentioned the fundraiser and asked her to stand by in case we needed her."

"Fanny Newhart. Do I know her?"

"Yeah, she's Grace's friend, the event planner. You met her at one of Ursula's dinner parties, the blonde married to the pilot. Anyway, she gave Grace a list of possible venues for the shower, and of course Lady Simpleton gave her the whole, 'Oh I want it to be small, just a few people, nothing fancy, blah, blah, blah …'"

Uh oh. Sylvia's engine is starting to rev up. Maybe I shouldn't have given her caffeine. I feel her one-woman comedy act is about to start.

"Long story short, Fanny offered to have an intimate lunch at her mega hacienda of a home in the Gables, and Grace jumped at it. Works out for Fanny too since she's about fourteen months pregnant and not very eager to run around town too much. Now, two things we know we must have are lychee martinis and great desserts. We'll see about food later. Figure about twenty people."

"No-brainer. Her colors are red and gold, I assume?"

"Ha! Red and gold. Real understated, right?" We both chuckle. "I've never met a woman who had to be pushed into the excitement of planning her own wedding." *Vroom, vroom* goes that engine. "I swear sometimes I want to shake her! 'Hey, wake up in there!'" She knocks on the side of her head as if it were a door. "YOU'RE GETTING MARRIED, HELLO!"

I can't take it anymore. I put my coffee cup down and break into laughter.

"Listen, she's going to enjoy this whether she likes it or not," Sylvia goes on. "She'll thank us later. We need to drag her into bride mode kicking and screaming if necessary."

I feel a stitch in my side from laughing so hard. When I double over, Sylvia stops her rant for a second, and then explodes in self-deprecating chortles.

Bruno walks in as we both attempt to recover and dry our teary eyes. "You ladies are having too much fun in here." He smiles warmly. "Jo, I'm heading out to get some lunch and I'm taking the staff roster with me to work on next week's schedule. You want anything?"

"Nah, I'll go raid Chef Manc's fridge. Take your time, things are slow right now." Bruno salutes and disappears. "Are you sure you don't want to have a quick bite, Sylvia?"

"Oh gosh, I was having so much fun I forgot my stupid lunch meeting. Ugh!" She slings her bag on her shoulder, and just as she's about to kiss me good-bye, she stops and holds my arms tightly. "I have a great idea! Why don't you come with me?"

"What? Are you nuts? I don't want to tag along on your meeting. The third-wheel hat doesn't look good on me."

"Oh yeah, of course, 'cause this is a date. No, woman, you're my friend. He wants to know what my life is all about, and my friends are important to me, so let him meet my fabulous friend the chef." She's very persuasive, but I'm on to her.

"Sylvia?" I sit on the corner of my desk and wait for her to come clean. After a few seconds of holding each other's gazes, she caves.

"Oh all right!" She throws her hands in the air and rolls her eyes. "Please come with me. I just don't want to go by myself. I don't like this guy, and I'm afraid I'll either be bored senseless or annoyed to the edge of murder. Come on,

Brooklyn, you said it yourself, things are slow around here and you have to eat anyway. Let Tony Reporter-Dude put it on his expense account."

"If you dislike this guy so much, why did you agree to do the piece?"

"I don't know, I like that they're showcasing women. There isn't a lot of that in media unless you're a movie star."

I'm not convinced. Her words make sense, but I get the feeling that there's more hidden in the shadows of this interview. I've never known Sylvia to need backup when it comes to business endeavors. My curiosity is piqued.

"Okay, whatever. Let me get out of my kitchen clothes." She gives me a look that combines triumph, relief, and gratitude. "So where are we eating?"

"Ortanique."

"The Caribbean place? Wow! Not bad, but pricey, though. Whose idea was that?"

"Mine, of course. He gave me carte blanche to pick the spot, and I figure he's gotta make it worth my while."

"They serve an outstanding beef filet with truffle cheese that I wouldn't mind trying, especially if someone else is paying."

"Honey, you can have two of them just for coming with me." She wraps her arms around me and I can't help getting that strange feeling again that the scope of her gratitude contradicts her indifference toward this interview. Or this interviewer.

"Syl, are you okay? You're so quiet."

"Oh, yeah, I'm fine, just a little tired from all that talking and full from all that food. I'm sorry it took so long, Jo."

"That's okay, I'm glad I came. He's a very interesting guy, isn't he?"

"Is he? I didn't pick up on anything extraordinary." Her eyes are glued to the road ahead as she drives me back to work.

"Are you kidding? All those kids he sponsors, the work he did with Spielberg for his Holocaust foundation. I was impressed. Come to think of it, we found out just as much about him as he did about you."

"I suppose. He was very eager to share details of his own life. Quite a different approach to interviewing, if you ask me."

"Ah come on, he was just trying to be casual and open. I don't know why you don't like him. Obviously, he likes you."

"WHAT? What do you mean? What are you saying?" She turns to me suddenly and brakes a little too roughly at the stop sign.

"Relax, all I'm saying is that he admires you, he has respect for you and what you have done with your magazine. What's wrong with you?"

"Nothing. I thought you meant …"

"You thought I meant he *likes you* likes you, right? I'll tell you what, I'll pass him a note in science class and find out. Oh please, Sylvia, how old are you? And so what if he *is* attracted to you? What's the big deal? If you don't feel the same way, no skin off your back, and if you do … Ohhh, I see." At last, the light of understanding shines on me.

Of course. It's as clear as a good diamond. Her discomfort during lunch every time he smiled at her. She barely touched her grouper, and didn't order dessert, a woman whose love for food is nothing less than sybaritic. Her clipped speech when answering questions, her natural eloquence all but gone. He tried once and again to reach her, but she wasn't having it. I was almost embarrassed to watch her behave like a spoiled child. He was enchanting, though. I was beginning to believe that men like Tony didn't exist anymore. Handsome, but not pretty. Witty, but with an unpretentious humor. Obviously smart, but without flaunt.

"What? You see what?" She stares at me and apparently has momentarily forgotten that she is driving.

"Eyes on the road, lady. You *do* like him!"

She grunts. "Huh! Now something's wrong with you. Are you on drugs?"

"Well, at least you're intrigued. You may be a crackerjack editor, but you're cellophane when it comes to emotions. He's rattled you and it's all over your face and your body language. I think you should go out with him and find out more.

"GO OUT WITH HIM?" Now she guffaws spectacularly and shifts uneasily in her seat while trying to keep just enough attention on driving to prevent us from crashing into the car ahead. "I … I'm not going anywhere with him! There is *no* way … I can't stand him!"

"Okay, okay, Mama Drama, don't go out with him. But you're gonna have to see him again about the project. See how you feel then."

She looks at me as if I've turned into a sci-fi monster right before her eyes.

After several attempts at formulating a coherent sentence, she whispers with a lump of emotion in her throat, "Please don't say anything to the other girls."

I make a cross over my heart with my index finger. "Promise. Not a word. So … how did you like your Costa Rican grouper?"

*I*t was a good idea on paper. At twenty-two years of age and after four years of dating, Jimmy Rosales decided we should get married because he was joining the army and he wanted me with him. But he didn't ask me first, he asked my mother. He thought it would be a gallant gesture, and it was, but he wasn't prepared for the reaction he got. My mother sat him down at the kitchen table in our small Brooklyn apartment, and gave him a concentrated look, like the Godfather about to tell some lackey that he's disappointed with his performance.

"Listen to what I gotta tell you, Jimmy. Are you sure you wanna do this? Do you know what you're getting yourself into?"

"Course I do, Ma. I've been with Jo since she was sixteen. I know what's what." He leaned back on his chair, slowly, meditating on whether he believed his own words.

"She's my daughter and I love her, but she ain't easy. She's got a brick for a head, and she wants things her way, or you're out on the street."

"Why you telling me this? You trying to scare me away?"

"No, but I don't want you to get into something you can't handle and have it blow up in your face. I always said it would take a big man to pair up with Jo."

"I can handle Jo," he said, puffing up his chest.

Naturally, I didn't find out about this conference until years later, and so we got married, and Jimmy Rosales began his fruitless attempt at "handling" me. I should give him credit, though, because he gave it a hell of a try. But I wasn't having any of it. Don't get me wrong, I was an acquiescent wife, gave him two kids, cooked, cleaned, laundered, moved every time he got new orders. At least I got to see the world and polish the Brooklyn Puerto Rican in me a bit, including the accent, before he retired and we settled in Miami. But when I had to call a spade a spade, nothing could stop me, not then, not now. When we were stationed in Germany and I said I wanted to go to culinary school when we got back to the states, he hollered and slammed things because he said my attention should be on taking care of the babies and him, and if I wanted to learn how to cook, I had a perfectly good stove at home. I wouldn't budge. The hunger inside me for something that was mine alone, something I didn't have to share credit for, tormented me. When I said I wanted no more children after Junior, he insulted me, berated me, he tried to guilt me into compliance, but we had no more children. Not an endearing quality in the wife of a Brooklyn tough guy.

After twenty-five years of marriage, he broke. He couldn't take what he thought of as insubordination, and he found comfort and submission in a coworker with flaming red hair, promptly divorced me, and now I am left with an undefined life. I met this man when I was a child, married him when I was barely a woman. Until I started culinary school while we were stationed in Fort Bragg, my life consisted of nothing more than orbiting around Planet Jimmy Rosales.

Now what? Who am I? What's my purpose? Jessica and Junior are grown and living their lives. I am forty-five years old, and I feel life outside my door pulling me to live it, summoning me to explore, but I don't even know how to start. I love being a pastry chef at Hotel St. Gabriel, and I'm darn good at it. I am in full and untainted control of my home and my finances. In many ways, I'm free. But there's still that longing for something more, I don't know what. It's not for a man. I'm smarter than that. It disturbs me to see how many women wander through their lives blind to their own identities in an endless and tortured wait for that heroic figure that will rescue them from obscurity. I am certain that I love myself enough to be my own hero.

I need to find the real Josephine Rosales (Marino, as soon as I get around to changing it legally) and fall in love with *her*. That's the kind of relationship I'm interested in having right now. And the ones I have with the foodie club. These women are phenomenal, and when I'm with them, I feel phenomenal—again.

A wallflower I am not, that's established. Even back in high school I was a magnetic force to which many were attracted. But if you approached, you had to be prepared to deal with the truth, good or bad, delivered to you with the power of a tsunami. If I liked you, you knew it. If I didn't, I'd tell you so you wouldn't live with any doubts. You either loved me or you hated me. I left no room for lukewarm feelings because I would not be ignored. That's just me.

Ironically, a lot of people liked me, admired me even. I suppose people are drawn to personalities that provoke visceral reactions in them. Who knows? I don't remember ever being a lost teenager without an identity, emulating others in search of a persona that would suit me. Others copied *me*. Even my sister Jackie found herself living uncomfortably in my shadow, and feeling guilty for not being the example, as a proper older sibling should be. But Admiration has an evil twin called Envy and they always travel together.

I wasn't blind. I knew there were those around me who would've liked to see the mighty oak fall, and I had the smarts to initiate a preemptive strike if necessary.

That was all good, but bravado can thrust you upward to a steep place of pride in which choices can become fuzzy with the altitude, and a tumble can be life-altering.

I never liked Jimmy that much when we were young. I couldn't like him because he was a nonfactor for me. He was one of those kids from my neighborhood who had no significance in my world. He was vanilla to me. He was the stereotypical Puerto Rican youth, soft curls, tawny skin, smoldering brown eyes. A hundred like him lived on my block. His presence didn't add or take away from my life. Until the gauntlet was thrown. I should've walked away. I was better than that, but I had to take the challenge.

"Hey Jo, look over there. Isn't that Pauline?" I could feel Anna Maria's lips touching my ear, the music in the club was so loud.

"Yeah … ha! She must be wondering how we got in here." At sixteen, I had perfected the skill of getting myself and my friends into a handful of familiar Brooklyn clubs not suited for minors. I was taller than the average girl by at least two inches, even without the heels I always wore with baby socks. And my curves, poured into tight jeans, belied my youth astonishingly.

Pauline sauntered over to where we stood, her four inches of teased, black-tinted hair still not enough to reach my chin. "Hey, you guys, be careful. They got a bouncer looking around for fake IDs."

"I ain't worried. I know everyone here. It's cool. Unless someone rats." I gave her a piercing icy look. "I don't think anyone's gonna do that, *right*?" She couldn't hold my glare and retreated to her corner. I smirked with self-satisfaction.

"Who's that she's with? He's *fiiine*." Anna Maria strained to see in the smoky bluish darkness.

"I think it's Jimmy Rosales. I don't know for sure," I yelled in her direction after a perfunctory look across the dance floor.

"Oh snap … By the way, I still can't believe what that slob said about you."

Here we go. "Wha?"

"You know, that she could take any guy away from you if she wanted."

Now, I knew Anna Maria was trying to goad me. Why did I let her?

"Oh yeah? She don't know what she's saying. She's full of crap." I took a slow sip of my illicit rum and Coke. I felt the hairs on the back of my neck begin to rise.

"You should go over there and vamp some at Jimmy." Anna Maria laughed heartily at her own wickedness. "She'd go freakin' crazy!"

"Nah, not worth it." I was trying hard to purge my head of the idea that this skank had dared to compare herself to me. I silently chanted that it was just gossip and to let it go.

Ah, but the impetuosity of youth was too potent to resist. I handed Anna Maria my drink and charged forward, sidestepping the dancers on the floor, syncing my steps with the fitful pattern of the strobe light, and the disco ball as my beacon.

It was so easy I was actually a little disappointed. All it took was a slight bump, a gentle touch on his shoulder, a smile, and a sweet "sorry."

"Looking good there, Jo," he said in my ear.

"And you got great taste, Jimmy." I turned and leaned into him before sauntering away.

The next twenty minutes were a flash. I returned to Anna Maria and reclaimed my drink. After a muffled squabble with Pauline, Jimmy made a beeline to where I sat, and before my glass was empty, we left together, but not before I took one last glance at his ex-date and shot a victory smile at her. I'm not proud of that. Well, maybe just a little.

I didn't want anything from Jimmy except a ride home, but after that night, I had a hard time losing him. He was relentless in the face of brutal rejection, and it was impossible not to take notice of his perseverance, given all the options available to him at the tender age of eighteen. Little did I know that he had enlisted my mother's aid in his pursuit, a strategically brilliant move as she alone knows the location of all the buttons to press to bring down my walls.

Hoping she could inherit my popularity crown, my sister couldn't get me out of the neighborhood fast enough, and as far as my father was concerned, I couldn't do better than an army man.

I wonder if, in retrospect, any of them feel pangs of guilt for their endorsements of my union with Jimmy. It doesn't matter now. I don't know how yet, but I'm going to take this loss and turn it into a winning lottery ticket.

Mindy

•

"Good morning, everyone," the formidable Judge Beatriz Sandoval offers as she takes her seat at the bench.

Looking at it from a glass-half-full perspective, I am thankful that this case is about to close. A quick skim of my notes reminds me of the vitriolic mudslinging I've had to witness for the past two years while representing Mrs. Lina Vandenburg, estranged wife of a business consultant whose asset column ends in eight digits.

"I congratulate Mr. and Mrs. Vandenburg, as well as their respective counsel, for finally coming to a mutual, albeit not speedy, agreement and I must say I am relieved for all of us. Go ahead, Miss Johnson."

I shake off my drifting thoughts, and as instructed, I proceed to summarize the details of one more instance in which the sacred institution of marriage falls like a matchstick structure. All of us present, judge, plaintiff, defendant, opposing counsel, and myself, couldn't be more disinclined to listening, yet again, to a regurgitation of the venom spewed at each other by two people who over twenty years ago vowed never to do exactly what they are now doing. How does that happen?

"Please testify that this is your signature, Mrs. Vandenburg," I request of my client as I present the hundredth version, it seems, of the marital settlement agreement. She attests as previously scripted and rehearsed, and I continue with as brief a description of the MSA to the judge as I can get away with, knowing that everyone here is already painfully aware of what's in it.

I have to make a change in my life. I'm twenty-eight years old and every day I feel like I'm wearing an ill-fitting suit. There's this unrelenting discomfort with my days and myself that I can't kick. It's making me crazy, and I can't take it anymore.

I'm not cynical about love and such things. The fact is I'd like to be married and have a family someday, but I fear that every time I wrap up one of these acrimonious cases, a little morsel of my faith in romantic alliances of any kind breaks away. I like men, and contrary to what some of my more "seasoned" friends say, I know there are good ones out there. I've met some. My father, for one. In fact, both my parents provided me with a prototype of what a marriage should be, with imperfections and pitfalls, but based on solid commitment.

For me, men are like a decadent dessert. When I have a craving, I have one. Most of the time, I'm fine without the indulgence. I haven't, however, found a game changer, one worth a shift in the way my world tilts on its axis.

"Very well, it seems everything is finally in order." Judge Sandoval exhales noticeably after signing the final decree, closes the file, crosses her milk chocolate arms over it decisively, and addresses my client and her new ex-husband. "Please don't take this as condescension because it is not intended that way, but allow me to remind you that you still have an underage daughter, and for her sake I beg you to work on having a more civil relationship as you will have to parent her together. At times during this journey, both of you have taken turns at behaving in embarrassingly childish ways, and you will do her a great disservice if that is the example you provide. Remember, *she* is the child, not you. We are adjourned." And with a gentle tap of her gavel, this nightmare is over. She may not have intended to convey condescension, but her words were dripping with it.

From the courthouse steps, I watch my zillionaire client fade into the sunset in her chauffeur-driven black stallion Bentley, then close my eyes and breathe the warm air for just a second. When I return to the office there will be applause, backslapping, hand shaking, champagne, and accolades from every partner. After all, this case has just secured the firm of Wasserman, Katz & Soto, Attorneys at Law, lots of repeat business and golden referrals from Mrs. Vandenburg. Maddie's file also awaits. I don't understand how in this age of the disposable marriage, people still walk down the aisle without a prenup securely clenched between their teeth.

No, I don't think I'll go back to the office just yet. I think I've earned the luxury of sitting for a moment to watch the grass grow. When I do go back, the roller coaster will begin again entirely too soon, and this time the ride will involve my friend. I probably shouldn't have taken the case, but how could I say no? She seems so befuddled and unsure of every step.

I walk to the small park across the street from the courthouse. There are plenty of unoccupied benches, but I'd rather feel the coolness of the grass on my skin under the shade of a lush banyan tree. I see all the regulars as I plop myself on a tiny promontory—the hot dog vendor, the homeless man napping on his favorite bench, a couple of youngsters making out on a neighboring knoll, and an endless number of lawyers munching on hot dogs and pretzels, talking on their cell phones and fighting to keep their papers from blowing in the breeze. I actually know some of them, but I don't care if they see me. I sit on my carefully folded jacket and look up at the sunlight peeking between the leaves of the branches overhead. I wish I had accepted my little sister's invitation to take a vacation in Argentina. A little tango with a dark, brooding dancer is my kind of therapy, but I couldn't leave Maddie stranded. Besides, a trip to the Southern hemisphere is just a Band-Aid, not a cure.

There were warnings as early as the first day at the hallowed Harvard Law School, I admit, but I ignored them. I saw them. I was just too lazy to heed them. Grace asked me recently why I decided to go to law school, and the words that came out of my mouth saddened me. "My parents wanted me to be a lawyer." Possibly the worst reason to do anything.

School had always been easy for me, so easy that I coasted all the way through my undergraduate years even with a double major. That's not as good as it sounds. Not much challenged me enough to fan the fires of professional passion. With poli-sci, I just went through the motions, but with nonprofit management there was a spark. If it hadn't been for that, I might've quit, I fear. A hunger to serve settled in my gut, a social conscience, some call it. It gave my lackluster days a splash of meaningful color. It didn't, however, hold my attention well enough to keep me from taking some unhealthy detours.

I got a robust case of the college crazies. I engaged in most of the stereotypical activities: alcohol, pot, and lots and lots of sex. Hard drugs didn't hold any interest for me. I wanted to have fun, not be sick all the time. Alcohol did get the best of me a few times, but I drank smartly and developed a respectable tolerance. I used pot like ladies in the thirties used cigarettes—just to look cool depending on whose company I kept. Sex was the most fun. I had me some lovely boys to whom I will always be grateful for helping me make beautiful memories during those ambiguous years. Some are still my friends, although I doubt their wives and girlfriends know how close we were.

I feel a short vibrating pulse in my pocket, and I take out my cell phone only to realize that while in the midst of my reverie, I've missed half a dozen text messages. All but one are from my office, as I expected and will ignore until I'm good and ready. The last one is from Sylvia. "Remember dinner with the girls at 7:00 p.m. Call me when you can." I hadn't forgotten, but somehow the reminder lightens my mood. It is a happy circumstance that our little club had scheduled our next epicurean adventure for tonight. A sweet end to a sour day.

I don't know why I enjoy these women as much as I do, and I'm nearing the point where I will no longer question it. They are older than I am, but they are the women I spend most of my leisure time with other than my family. I have some friendly acquaintances in my age group, but they're exhausting with their romantic dramas or working mom guilt. I can't relate. An evening with the mature set always stimulates me, and almost always leaves me refreshed.

"Glad you called," Sylvia says. "You're the only vote missing. We couldn't decide on where to eat. Everyone has different hankerings today."

"What are the choices?"

"Okay, there's Café Prima Pasta, Tobacco Road, or The Palm. What's your pleasure?"

"So, Italian, burgers, or steak. Right now, I could eat all three," I say, suddenly noticing how hungry I am when my mouth begins to water. "I don't know about Tobacco Road. The music may be too loud to let us talk, and we need to catch up on the OVCC fund-raiser."

"Yep, that's true. Lots going on."

"I think I need some comfort food tonight, Sylvia, so I'm voting Italian."

"Rough day?"

"One of many lately."

"Well, I think you'll get your wish. Your vote makes it majority for pasta."

"How're we doing on ticket sales?"

"Nearing four hundred. At $250 a pop we already have enough to start on those priority repairs."

"Awesome. My only concern is that we've been so caught up with the people that can afford $250 for a dinner, that we haven't addressed others who may want to make smaller contributions. We need to have a plan for ongoing funding past this big fund-raiser."

"Sounds like you already have something in mind."

"Yeah, I think I do. We'll talk tonight."

"Okay, Mindy, see you at seven."

Whatever peckishness I felt has turned into ravenous hunger after all that talk of food. A hot dog will have to do. I walk toward the vending cart with a heavy heart as I return to the realities of the here and now. How many hours until dinner?

••

*T*here's so much going on with the décor at Café Prima Pasta—a forest of dark wood, endless black-and-white photography on the walls, ornate chandeliers hanging from ceilings—but you couldn't really categorize it as garish or erratic. It looks New Jersey Italian, unique and warm. This isn't a trendy yuppie spot at all. I like that. The patrons you may find on any given night make for a motley crowd. Sitting at the table behind us is a big guy drenched in gold jewelry and his two nubile dates, and right across from him sits a Cuban clan enjoying a family dinner. I can envision this place in a slick gangster movie where a "twenty-dollar handshake" with a smarmy host gets a shady character some type of special treatment. The glitz of it all and the jazz lounge music playing in the background make for the perfect atmosphere to wash away my day.

"At this point, I think we may be in over our heads." Sylvia dabs the ends of her mouth with refinement after a bite of her spinach-and-ricotta-stuffed pasta. "None of us are able to give this fund-raiser proper attention with full-time jobs and all, so Fanny agreed to oversee it provided she doesn't have to do too much legwork. I told her we'd all pitch in to help with that if necessary."

"How far along is she now?" I ask, staring at my voluptuous dish. I believe they used a whole cow to make my lasagna Bolognese. I'm so happy right now.

"Almost seven months, but she's so tiny, the big belly's already a little bothersome," Grace says. She's having one of her indecent affairs with her pear-and-prosciutto gnocchi. Watching her sop bread with every drop of vodka sauce is a trip. She's like a kid in a sandbox.

"I hooked her up with Ursula and it looks like our little tycoon is footing the bill for the open bar." Sylvia has now taken out her iPad and is reading bullet points from her ultra-organized to-do list for the project. I wish I could be like her, but that's why God created people like my assistant Nilda, to help the incurably muddled Mindys of the world.

"Are we done with ticket sales? I need a number fast. The event is in less than four weeks." Always cucumber-cool Jo seems a bit edgy. It can't be easy to serve a five-course meal to four hundred people all at once.

"Yup, we're done. Three hundred eighty-six is your number." Sylvia reads off the screen. "I emailed all of you Fanny's contact info so you can talk any specifics with her."

"So that puts us in the $100,000 neighborhood, gross. That's a pretty respectable neighborhood. Our expenses are minimal so it looks like our net will be generous." I must admit, secretly, I didn't think we'd do this well. I wonder how much of this is

Richard Montiel's influence, and if so, why? You couldn't pay me in gold bars to bring him up right now.

By my observation, Maddie and Grace seem on normal terms, so I assume Maddie's not aware of the delicate congress that took place recently between our friends and those she considers her enemies. I don't know the details of what transpired that evening, but everyone agreed it was Grace's place to tell her about the infamous dinner with Richard and Mercy, even with the certainty that her reaction would not be pleasant. I'm sure there was no malicious intent in the delay, but it's interesting. As ballsy as Grace is, I'm surprised she hasn't done it yet. Even more interesting is the fact that, obviously, Richard hasn't told her either. Grace should've talked to her before they met. Now it's just a weapon in his pocket. It's only a matter of time.

"So, Mindy, you said you had some ideas about more long-term fund-raising. We can't throw one of these hoedowns every month." Sylvia brings me back from my ruminations, and I continue wrangling my beefy lasagna.

"Yeah, I was thinking of creating a crowdfunding web page where people can go in and make donations of any size. We can put pictures and talk up the place and its contribution to the community. Not only will it allow those who can't pay $250 for a dinner plate to get involved, but it'll create more awareness. We should also mention the link in any advertising we're doing. The fund-raiser is a great kickoff, but this has to be an open-ended thing, or the center will fall through the cracks again."

"I've been thinking about that too." Peggy nods along in agreement as she revels in her Parmesan chicken. "I really think we're doing a good thing here, and I wouldn't want this to be a one-time effort. Don't you think it would be great if the center could offer some free counseling and maybe some legal services? There are a lot of low-income immigrant families in that area."

Peggy's words ignite something within. The idea of contributing to this cause from front and center rather than just from behind the scenes triggers a spontaneous warmth in the deepest parts of me.

"The legal would be easy. I don't mind committing a few hours a week for that, and I can probably recruit one or two additional attorneys."

"Well, then along those lines almost every one of us can provide some sort of service, and as awareness grows, others with different skills may want to volunteer. I can do some tutoring, and Jack can teach music lessons." Grace's visionary gears turn in unison with her fork, which has now become a pointer.

As I watch everyone's reactions, I realize I'm not the only one awakened by the notion of hands-on involvement. When did this community center become such a passion for us all? Up to now, Peggy was the only one who'd had any relationship with Ocean View. Perhaps each of us, in our own way, feels disenfranchised from the world and this project seems like a path toward connection, global and to each other.

"I could start a photography club." Sylvia offers with assenting nods rippling all around the table.

"That's a good idea, and you can ask Tony to join you and add videography to that," says Jo almost absentmindedly, as clearly most of her attention is centered on her creamy tortellini polka-dotted with green peas.

Suddenly, I notice Sylvia is frozen in her seat. Her wine glass is suspended midway between the table and her lips, which are now open almost as wide as her eyes as they stare at Jo directly across from her. There's been some sort of shift, I don't know what exactly.

"Who's Tony?" asks Maddie, her eyes ping-ponging from Sylvia to Jo.

"Nobody," Sylvia answers quickly as she takes a long and full chug of her wine.

"*Ooooh* … nobody? Yeah, right!" continues Maddie, picking up on Sylvia's not-so-subtle attempt at dismissing the question. "Who is it, Jo?"

Jo is now staring back at Sylvia, seemingly in shock. "Uh … he's … uh … just a colleague of Sylvia's I met. I think he's going to cover the fund-raiser for the magazine or something." She's answering Maddie's question, but her eyes haven't moved from Sylvia and her tone is almost apologetic. Now all of us are quiet and still. I wonder what the busboy filling our water glasses is thinking. No one is eating, no one is drinking, no one is talking. That doesn't happen often in this group. This Tony must be important.

"It's no one of significance, Madeline," Sylvia says in exasperation as she resumes eating, and the rest of us slowly follow. "He's a reporter from New York that I've been meeting with for interviews. His TV network is profiling me on some news magazine show they broadcast. He asked if he could help with the fund-raiser, and I told him he could contribute to the cause by bringing a camera crew and talking to some of the guests. That takes the pressure off me to find someone to cover the dinner. He offered, so why not take advantage if he wants to help."

"Is he your *date* for the evening?" Maddie asks in the tone of a seventh grader, a twinkle in her eye.

The loud clink from Sylvia slamming her utensils on the plate makes us all wince and stop eating—again. What's left of my lasagna is sad and cold and looks like the scraps from an autopsy now, but I still think this uncomfortable exchange between Sylvia and Maddie is even more unappetizing.

"It's business, Maddie, that's it. Quit reading any more into it." She makes a quick sweep around the table. "All of you, stop it." We all look at each other as if trying to confirm whether we're all indeed thinking the same thing. Except Jo. She has an anguished expression on her face and keeps her eyes locked on her nearly empty plate, hoping, it seems, to drown herself in the leftover cream sauce.

Sylvia tries to refocus on her food, but she too finds it unpalatable. She takes care to place her utensils delicately over her plate this time, removes the napkin from her lap, and begins to rise from her chair. "I'm sorry, I didn't mean to snap. I'm going to the restroom and girls, please, when I come back, can we get some dessert and talk about the fund-raiser? We have to pick the speakers and we don't have a lot of time."

We all nod fervently but no one dares to talk. "Dessert, YES!" I burst. Someone had to break the silence. It might as well be me, and dessert is definitely a catalyst for peace and harmony with this bunch. As we watch her walk away, I feel the tension subside, and just as we appear to be composing ourselves, Maddie leans conspiratorially into the table.

"So Jo, who's Tony?" We all look at her in wide-eyed disbelief that she could still linger on this topic, which has clearly made the evening beyond awkward. Without skipping a beat, a scolding and collective voice rings in unison.

"MADDIE!"

Grace

There's only so much a middle-aged bride can take. This morning I got a love text from the cake designer with estimate number four on a minimalist two-tier ivory wedding cake for twenty people. What's so complicated about that? The venue coordinator doesn't think she needs to answer my phone calls just because my October wedding is seven weeks away, and in the world of event planning, apparently that translates into seven centuries.

But the dress issue is a whole new kind of ugly. Crime-scene ugly. My dress makes my already prodigious breasts look like nuclear warheads, and the seamstress doing the alterations, who happens to have perfectly round and demure B-cups, keeps saying things like, "You look ethereal, you look angelic…" *Pu-leeze*. I look like a huge marshmallow.

I admit I was quite reluctant to search for a dress, but the moment I saw this one, I knew the universe could now rest at ease.

After the last failed attempt at finding this elusive gown with assistance from my friends, I designed an action plan. I had only a small window of time to decide, so I gave myself a deadline to accomplish my clandestine mission. I say clandestine because from the moment I realized the ladies and I had different visions for my wedding, their opinions were no longer sought. If I couldn't upgrade from the pretty little white sundress already in my closet at a reasonable price and within reasonable time from the big day, the operation would be aborted.

Two days before the deadline, I felt an odd mixture of regret and relief that I had not been successful in my quest. Some dresses were too elaborate, some were too simple, a large number were too expensive, and the majority just didn't look right on me. So I pulled my sundress out of the closet, as I had done every time I came home empty-handed from hunting. And every time I looked at it, it seemed more and more radiant, elegant, and tailored. It would do. It would *have* to do.

But I still needed shoes. I'd looked around while chasing the dress and found that I was always drawn to strappy, rhinestoned sandals. Since this was definitely going to be my last wedding, and it seemed I wouldn't be shelling out any money on a dress, I decided to indulge in a pair of divine Ferragamo pale gold sandals artfully bejeweled with the most delicate of crystal flowers that haunted my dreams since the first time they twinkled at me.

As I waited behind a customer at the checkout counter of the exclusive little shoe boutique, I observed, as is my hobby on those rare occasions when I venture into such uppity establishments, the behavior of what I consider more evolved (meaning richer and prettier) members of my gender. I don't feel posh enough to shop in these places. I'm always afraid I'm going to have a *Pretty Woman* moment, and some saleswoman will look me up and down with scorn and tell me, "We don't have anything for you here."

On this day, however, I had an eye-opening revelation as I narrowly evaded an attack by a rogue, unmanned Lacoste stroller. Its escaped passenger was a toddler wearing a Kermit green shirt with a matching little alligator embroidered on his chest, who was being chased, and ultimately caught, by his five-foot-nine, raven-haired, emerald-green-eyed, size-zero, twentysomething mommy.

As she wiped her sweaty forehead with the back of her hand after hog-tying the Lacoste imp back into the stroller, she offered a general apology. Then she went on to express her anguish to her companion, another excruciatingly gorgeous alien from their planet, about possibly being late to dinner since they still needed to stop at Fendi to buy some filler paper for their cool retro day planners. I guess they don't have Office Depot on Planet of the Greek Goddesses. All this, I noticed, as she waited to pay for a $1,700 nylon handbag that was probably made in China for pennies.

I learned that day that this more "evolved" group contains idiots just like any other subset of society. I shook my head and chuckled in my mind as I left the shop satisfied at having made some progress on the issue of wedding attire and feeling a little more evolved myself.

But then, the day got even better. I looked for a break in the traffic flow to cross Miracle Mile, wedding dress mecca in Miami, when suddenly I saw it. In a small vintage store, diagonally opposite to where I stood—a gossamer vision in the most immaculate shade of ivory. It beckoned to come closer. Had I not been standing at that precise angle, I might not have seen it, for it wasn't overtly displayed in the window. It stood next to the shop counter where a store clerk adjusted its shimmering cap sleeves on an undeserving, unimpressed, lifeless, headless mannequin with no appreciation for the splendor that embraced it.

I don't remember exactly how and when I crossed the street, spellbound as I was, but I'm grateful to all the motorists who didn't run me over. When I touched the nearly translucent chiffon, tears burned my eyes. When I traced the silk satin detail that gathered at the bustline to define the empire waist, I wept with joy. And when the saleswoman told me the astonishingly reasonable price, I threw my arms around her.

Even in the awkward sample size, I believed I had never looked more radiant. Thoughts about troublesome fittings to come never entered my mind. I swayed in it for what seemed an eternity. At last, I was able to whisper the words.

"I'm a bride!"

••

Remembering the day I found my wedding gown is a good way to soothe the despair I feel about my first fitting. I was so in love that day, it never occurred to me that this sheath of magnificence might not just supernaturally enfold every stretch of my body, the smooth corners as well as the questionable alleys, with unconditional perfection.

Now, I sit on the couch, almost in a fetal position, choking the stuffing out of a throw pillow, trying to follow along with the New York Yankees on TV. I strain to focus all my powers of concentration on every play and every cryptic sign exchanged between pitcher and catcher to settle myself and stifle the instinct to scream in panic.

Thank God for the Yankees and for my unmitigated love for them, a vestigial remnant of my Long Island roots. And because Jack can smell sports in the air, he comes out of the bedroom where he's been decompressing, as he calls it, after his workday. I call it napping. His curiosity is fueled not by loyalty to my team but simply by the fact that there are males playing with a ball on the screen.

He notices that more pressing than the bases-loaded-two-outs drama on TV is the dread apparently manifested on my face.

"It's baseball, not a horror movie," he teases tentatively.

"My fitting was a disaster. The dress looked so much nicer on the mannequin. Why didn't I notice that when I tried it on? Is it too late to elope?" My thoughts spill out unrestrained.

Jack winces. "It can't be that bad. What's wrong with it?"

"No, I don't think I can say any more. I may start crying and who knows when I'll stop, or I may give away too many details about the dress and have to kill you later." I sink back into the couch and continue murdering the pillow.

How can planning such a small-scale wedding reduce an otherwise intelligent, reasonable woman into a whimpering, pitiful creature with the backbone of a slug?

"I'm going to work on next semester's syllabus. Another ulcer in the making. Oh, I feel a headache coming on. This wedding madness is just too much." I stand and chuck the strangled pillow carcass.

"How do you know it's not the syllabus instead of the wedding that's causing the headache?" Bless him, he's trying to make another joke.

"Because every time I think about that dress, I start doing head slaps and asking *why, why, why are we doing this?*" I say more harshly than intended.

He looks downhearted. I think I've hurt his feelings. He wants me to enjoy this process, but he can't possibly understand. He's just wearing linen pants and a shirt. He's done. No makeup, no hairstyling, no nosy, opinionated friends who caused all this trouble in the first place.

I sit back down next to Jack, put my arms around his shoulders, and lean my head against his cheek.

"I guess this would not be a good time to tell you that the cake woman needs to talk to you again," he says softly, rubbing my arm as he delivers the message.

"That's okay," I sigh and laugh miserably. "I'm going to turn Fanny loose on her. She promised if anyone gave me grief, she'd use the .357 Magnum she has locked and loaded under her bed. What a terrifying thought."

For no-nonsense event planning, Fanny is at your service. Some women scrapbook, some do yoga. Fanny Newhart, party planner extraordinaire, likes big guns and fast cars. Besides the Magnum, she owns a 9 mm Glock and a Colt .45. She is fully licensed to own each one and has thorough training in how to use them, which is pretty much all she ever got from her cop ex-husband. And every car I've ever seen her drive looks like a time traveling DeLorean, flux capacitor included.

Mind you, she is five foot three, not much over one hundred pounds, with naturally flaxen hair, milky white skin, and crystalline blue eyes with just the right number of pale freckles flawlessly placed on her cheeks. Mata Hari disguised as Doris Day. An ingénue packing heat.

She's been married now for three years to Reese Newhart, a pilot for a Scandinavian airline who looks like the perfect blend of Dwayne "The Rock" Johnson and Bradley Cooper. In spite of his rugged, hunky appearance though, he is the sweetest, earthiest guy, which I think is what truly makes him remarkable.

It amazes me how different all my friends are. On the surface, it would seem I'm the only commonality between them. Friendship is amorphous, I find. It's fluid, unstructured, and mystical. It follows no rules. In my comeback into the world of female bonding, I've been drawn toward forging liaisons with personalities that are categorically opposed to each other.

To the same degree that petite Fanny is transparent, Maddie is ambiguous. To say you see only the tip of that iceberg is a huge understatement. She will deny this passionately and insist that she is an open book. Yet, every time I spend time with her, regardless of how much I enjoy her company, I always leave with the impression that something has been withheld. I wouldn't call her mysterious. I would characterize it more as having endless layers, too many to sift through.

Which brings me once again to a predicament that has me in agony every day for several reasons. First, the memory of that excruciatingly awkward dinner at the Deauville with Rich and Maddie's replacement is not one that I wish to conjure.

Then, there's the baffling fact that Mercy was hard to hate. I tried my darndest not to find her charming and funny, and to deny how suited to each other they seem. I wanted to believe it reprehensible that Rich has never looked happier or more relaxed. And finally, there is the uncomfortable fact that Maddie doesn't know about this dinner, and I haven't had the rum balls to tell her.

I wish Rich hadn't become such a visible part of this fundraiser. The question of why he's so involved gnaws at me. Let's just say altruism is not his highest priority. The Montclair agenda is always at the core of all his actions from what I've observed. I don't think his objective is to hurt Maddie deliberately, so all I can come up with is that he wants his not-so-new relationship legitimized, and if he has to buy such validation, then that's what he'll do. The fact that this has all but destroyed Maddie's identity and made her erratic and insecure is perhaps lost to him. Or I hope it is. I imagine his ego is bruised after his repeated yet useless attempts at reconciling with Maddie, but I refuse to entertain the possibility that he might be that diabolical.

Ordinarily, I have no qualms about telling people whatever truths they need to hear, even to my own detriment. I just don't know which Maddie I will get once I drop the bomb. Will it be the forgiving Maddie, the indignant, betrayed Maddie, or the wounded, I'm-such-a-victim, everything-happens-to-me Maddie? It's the last one I don't want to face. That Maddie is intractable and unreasonable. It's her default personality and I don't want to enable it.

I have three choices and none of them attractive. I can wait until Maddie finds out about the dinner through a third party, and then play it down as inconsequential when she confronts me. After all, it was just business and everyone who knows can corroborate that I went under duress. Not a chance. There is no way that this can be seen as trivial. I could ignore it and hope that it will never come out. That is as likely to happen as me being conveniently abducted by aliens. Too many people know and are waiting for it all to hit the fan. I guess it must be door number three. I have to tell her myself. Frightful choice.

I should've done it right after that night, or better yet, I should've given her a heads-up. The timing is lousy right now. Too much going on with the benefit coming up soon, then the bridal shower and the wedding. Odds are great that she will shut down and distance herself from all the events either out of anger or just to be passive-aggressive.

Come to think of it, the benefit may work in my favor. Maybe I don't have to tell her right away. Maybe I can put it off. Everyone is so busy getting ready, it could buy me some time, and that momentum may even carry until after the wedding. I can hope, right? Yeah, I hoped for my fitting to be a thrilling moment and look how that turned out. What are the chances that I would miscalculate twice in one day? Very good chances, actually.

•••

"Brian and I broke up and I'm moving to California, Mom." As if my day hadn't been tormenting enough, now this. Just like that. No sugarcoating, no attempt to soften the blow. A bit of defiance, even. I don't know how to respond. I have to tread lightly.

"Wow, what happened?"

"Nothing in particular. It's just been unraveling for a while. We're both over it." *Youth.*

"So what's in California?"

A heavy pause and an equally heavy sigh. "Dad's been there for a while now and he says he can help me get a good job at his bank seeing as I speak decent Spanish."

"California …" I say wistfully. "And I thought Daytona Beach was far."

"I know, but I gotta do something. Florida's got nothing for me anymore. I've lived here all my life. I'm tired of it, and I want to try something new."

"When's the move?"

"Next week. Brian has friends over there that he wants to visit, so he's driving me and my stuff in his van."

I'm fighting hot tears as I hear my only child so bluntly inform me over the phone that she's getting as far away from me as the borders of the continental United States will allow.

I have nothing to lose, so I'll extend one last olive branch for the sake of a peaceful good-bye.

"Are you sure you don't want to wait a few more weeks and come to the wedding?"

More silence and now a sigh that sounds laden with irritation. "I can't, Mom. Dad already made arrangements for an interview at the bank. I gotta get out there. Sorry. Besides, you said it wasn't gonna be a big event."

"Oh, it's not … at all." *I still wish you would be there.* "It's okay. You're right. If there's a good opportunity, you should look into it right away." That's the best I can do at pretending to be supportive. "So would you like Jack and me to drive up this weekend and bring you some of the stuff you left in your closet?"

"Really? That would be awesome! I'll take you guys to lunch at this place on the beach. Jack'll love it."

"Great. I'm excited!" I'm not, but if enthusiasm is what she needs from me right now, then there it is. As if I could tell her what I really feel. *Don't go, Lily. I want you here, close to me, so I can put you in a glass case where no one can hurt you. Remember your father never gave a flip about you when you were little, dear.*

My daughter Lily has many of my good qualities, some of my bad ones, and one that she brought to the table on her own: She is pathologically stubborn. I'm sure there are other people in the world as stubborn as she, but I've never met any.

My use of the word "pathologically" is not dramatic exaggeration. It is a painful fact that Lily's hardheadedness has a severely unhealthy impact on all those who surround her and can be crushing to those who love her. Not to mention how it complicates her own life.

When she was thirteen years old and brought me a report card that had been blatantly doctored, she defiantly assured me that she hadn't done it even after I spoke to her teacher and confirmed the B in math was really a D. No matter how much leniency I promised or how much punishment I threatened, she wouldn't admit to the deed. I don't know whether I was more awestruck by the obstinacy or disturbed by the outright lie.

I'm not privy to many details of her relationship with Brian the Hippie, but I do know it takes two to make any kind of relationship, and two to break it. Not that I'm devastated by that bit of news. Brian's a good twenty-four-going-on-sixteen kid, but Lily is light-years more mature. Jack and I always thought he held her back from discovering the bright fire that we know lives inside her.

What a difference it would make in her life if she used that implacability to her benefit. Her life has not been easy since she left home, but I have to give her credit. Even in the darkest of times, she's never asked me for a penny or an ounce of help. Any time I've lent a hand, it's been on my initiative. It's that fire that can turn her dark mullishness into productive tenacity. I wish she could see it.

If I had to guess, I would say Brian's slacker, mama's-boy ways were his contribution to the breakup, and I would bet money Lily's stubbornness was hers.

So, trying to list the reasons why a move to the other side of the country is a decision that warrants some time and careful consideration would be reverting to my old habits with Lily. And then she would react as was *her* habit. She would put a virtual rocket up her backside and fly away even faster.

More disturbing even is this new relationship she has established with her once-estranged father. In my unrelenting cynicism, I question the motives on both sides. I've known for a while that he has been trying to creep back into her life since she moved away from Miami, but Lily would not tear down the walls until now. The breakup and the uncertainty of taking her life on a new course, and being back in survival mode, as she has been often since she left home, have weakened her defenses. Now Dad's found a crack in the fortress into which he could squirm.

I can't help wondering why he now pursues her with such zeal when he couldn't be bothered as she was growing up. It could be remorse, or maybe it's the empty nest syndrome. He spent the better part of Lily's life raising his new wife's children, and now that they're grown and gone, he may want to fill the void with his own child. Or maybe it's because his health has faltered over the years, and he feels the urgency to make good on responsibilities unfulfilled. Whatever his reasons, I'm sure there's something in it for him. If you look deep enough, you will always find a self-serving objective for all he does.

Yes, I sound vindictive and jealous, but who can blame me? I raised the child alone, I had no help, no respite from being the bad guy. I shudder at the memory of how many nights I cried myself to sleep from guilt and sorrow after disciplining her for this or that infraction. Now most of them seem insignificant. I never felt I could let my guard down for fear my strong-willed child would stray from what I thought was the righteous path to success. And the mornings after were even more painful because then I had to face my baby's injured looks of mistrust and desolation. She was never one to talk back to me, or scream that she hated me, or throw tantrums. But her silences were so much more agonizing.

Now, after she's grown, and armed with tools I gave her to be independent and discerning, he gets to enjoy her age of discovery with none of the labor pains, and I'm left behind on the dark side of the moon.

But high above the bitterness, the feeling of abandonment, the sense of unfair irony, and the deep gash in my heart inflicted by the vast distance that will now separate us, is my indefatigable desire for Lily to have a joyful life and her soul to be at peace. I will pray for that, no matter what the cost. If reuniting with her father will bring healing to the angry little girl inside her, if he finally takes her under his wing to protect and help her find her way as a father should, and I must step aside for a while, I will do so with a wounded yet glad heart. In fact, to see her happy and successful will be ample payment for my sacrifice, and perhaps then my time in the prison of guilt will finally be done.

My mother is fond of telling the story of how, when I was a little girl, my way of playing with dolls consisted of moving them from one place to the other by dragging them by the hair. She would patiently show me how to change my doll's clothes, and caress her, and give her kisses just like a baby. When the demonstration was over, I would look at my mother and the doll, and proceed to firmly grab on to a handful of the doll's hair and go on my merry way. Thanks, but no thanks. It was simply not my style. Sometimes when I flash back to the dark days of the war between Lily and me, I see that my style didn't change that much when I became a mother.

The result is that now, against my strongest instincts, I must curb the impulse to give advice that is not solicited, anesthetize my feelings to protect them, and yield to maintain diplomatic relations with my child.

I'm surprised Lily still has hair because all my dolls ended up bald.

Madeline

•

I love the smell of the ocean in Miami. This is what I call "aromatherapy." Sultry and sweet at the same time; mangoes, coconuts, and salinity mixed in a provocative fragrance.

The southernmost point in Miami Beach is a prime spot for people-watching. And beautiful-people-watching at that. Something about the cobalt sea in the background accentuates the sheen on bronze skin, moist from surf and sweat.

On most days, the scene is reminiscent of a supermodel photo shoot. Supple, fat-free human shapes stretch to hit a volleyball over a net, drift on the wet sand, or simply adorn the seashore while sun-worshipping under the swaying palm trees, mojito in hand. If you're lucky, on any given day you may even spot a vacationing movie star or one of those pseudo-celebrities whose only claim to fame seems to be getting their picture taken on a red carpet.

Today is Monday; the place is quiet and there is only a sprinkle of people spread over the narrow infinity of the sandy strip. Still, seagulls squawk their displeasure at the human intrusion. After an enormous effort to keep it together long enough to drop off the kids at summer day camp, I kept driving on and on, aimless, until I reached water. I feared that if I drove home, I would sit and choke on my own bile, or worse even, detour straight to the college and confront Grace.

This is better. Walking by the ocean always helps me think. I have to do something. This is one calamity I won't be able to delegate to the heavens, considering I talk to Grace almost daily. Not to mention we have to communicate about the benefit, the bridal shower, and the wedding coming up. I don't know about the last two. It's not looking good right now.

It is a sweltering hot day, but it's the stinging heat of anger that overtakes me, heat that comes roaring from within and pushes me into darkness even as I walk under the incandescent sun. I thought after I slept the hair-pulling phase of my rage would subside, and I'd be able to make some sense of the whole thing. But my sleep was restless at best, and my anger is still solid. It hammers on my bewildered mind, each painful strike a promise of another to follow. Mental images of Grace's betrayal try in vain to escape. My heart convulses, and in the brightness of the revelation, breaks into lifeless pieces.

Grace is not my friend, she can't be. Why didn't she tell me? I had to find out from the whore herself. Grace pretty much handed that demon the opportunity to stab me in the heart. Maybe I'm overreacting. Maybe having the whole adulterous mess thrown in my face yet again stirred up all the original anger, and I'm taking it out on Grace because I can no longer punish Rich. But no matter what spin I try to put on it, I can't find a justifiable reason why Grace would leave me so vulnerable. It's not her way. She walks around self-righteously professing to be the most genuine of humans, and she does this?

I got caught with my britches down, as they say. Yesterday had been relatively pleasant and productive, and although I was expecting the now habitual discomfort of receiving my daughter from Rich after one of her Daddy Sundays, this particular Sunday blindsided me.

After watching David's baseball game, I dropped him off at the pizza place where the team was celebrating their victory. A few of his teammates had planned to catch a movie after the game, and suddenly I had the opportunity for some much-needed solitude. Several months have now gone by since the demise of my home life as it once was, and I feel stronger and able to spend time with myself without fearing our empty house.

I was sitting on my bed, laptop on lap, an island surrounded by a sea of cookbooks and interior design magazines, when the doorbell rang. Iris sprang into the foyer, gloriously disheveled, sandy all over, her cheeks rosy from the sun. But Rich wasn't with her. Mercy was.

"Hi Mommy, I'm back!"

"Hi precious, did you have a nice time?" It took superhuman will to keep my focus on Iris and not on the vile creature now inside my house.

"Yup, the beach was awesome! Dad rented a jet ski. It was soooo cool! I think I want one."

"Oh, okay," I laughed. "I'll get my magic wand." Iris giggled too and I noticed the whore laughing softly along with us. Mercy stood at a short distance, respectfully waiting for the mother-daughter greetings to be over. Why was she here? What twisted game was Rich playing? How could he send her into my inner sanctum? I thought I should acknowledge her presence.

"Hi, Mercy, thanks for bringing her home. Where's Rich?" I think I said the words as I signaled to Iris in the direction of the stairs. Hopefully she'd think to make a beeline for the shower, but I wasn't holding my breath.

"I asked him to let me bring Iris this time."

We looked at each other for a few seconds, and over the silence I heard the stomping of the proverbial elephant in the room.

"Well?" I asked, eager to end the suspense.

She shifted her body uncomfortably and gave me a pained look. "Maddie, I bet you won't believe this, but I never intended to hurt you. I've spent many days tortured over how this all went down."

I crossed my arms at my chest and looked down at my toes to gather myself and not allow my baser instincts to take over, because at that moment I wanted to deck her, right there in my house.

"*You've* been tortured? Oh wow, I didn't know. I'm so sorry you've had to suffer through this." I guess I didn't do a good job of keeping my composure. "Well, I do take comfort in the fact that my husband was there with a good screw every time you needed consoling." I wanted to scream but my voice was a furious whisper because Iris was within earshot.

"I shouldn't've said anything," Mercy said, shaking her head and taking a step back. "I thought enough time had passed and you'd be receptive, but I see that you're not. Forgive me, please … for everything."

"There will be snow in hell when I forgive you, and make no mistake—if there is a God in heaven, you will both live to regret what you did." My heart was pounding hard at my rib cage, desperate to break free. "Already you're in for a rude awakening because Rich is no prize, the lying scumbag. But I guess you two are perfect for each other."

"Okay, Madeline, I get it. I'm going. My apology was sincere, but I won't stand here and be your punching bag." She turned toward the door and then she stopped and looked at me again, but this time the passive expression had become determined. *She'd better leave now*, I thought. *I'm not made for this. I don't want to say any more.*

"By the way, say hi to Grace for me. Tell her I hope she has a beautiful wedding day."

My heart stopped its frantic pounding and dropped to my gut like a rock. "How do you know Grace?" I asked, my tone accusatory and territorial.

"Oh, didn't she tell you? Rich and I had dinner with her and her fiancé a couple of weeks ago to discuss the community center benefit. They were very appreciative for our help. They're lovely people. I can see why you love her so much." And with that, she slithered out the door.

The blow had knocked me clear off the ground, as if vicious arms had pushed me into a black precipice, and yet my body was frozen in place, staring at the space where she once stood a second ago, when life still made some sense. Betrayal has a friendly face.

••

*T*he beach served its purpose. By the time I pull into the mall parking lot, the nausea is under control, my rosacea is no longer an angry red but a pale pink, and I've stopped shaking every time I picture my once-upon-a-time friend Grace on a double date with my archenemy. I'm dizzy with the swirling questions in my head. She said it was to "discuss the community center benefit," so why wouldn't Grace tell me about it? Would I feel any different if she had told me? Why couldn't Jack and Rich meet without making it a cozy couples dinner? Oh Grace, if only you'd told me.

The conflagration in my heart and mind is beginning to settle, and I think I can try to come up with a reasonable course of action. Some retail therapy will also improve my perspective. It always does. One look at my overburdened, parlor-sized walk-in closet, and you can tell what kind of a year I've had.

First things first. I have to return Mindy's call. She wants to give me an update on the divorce, and this misery inside me will turn me ruthless if she gives me bad news. I'm not in the mood to compromise. Well, I don't really know how to be ruthless, but at least I'll try to be tough. Maybe I'll get her advice on what to do about Grace. No. I'm not telling anyone about this just yet. I'm not sure who my friends are anymore.

A full bar was a nonnegotiable factor when Mindy and I decided where to meet for lunch. She graciously agreed to meet me at Carpaccio in the Bal Harbour Shops, and when she arrives, I'm already halfway through what I know will be only my first glass of raspberry-scented Beaujolais Régnié.

I've managed to raise my spirits by dropping just a couple thousand at my new best friend, Prada, and the European energy and happy bustle of shoppers and patrons is a welcome distraction. I even get a little naughty amusement from watching some Euro-trashy broads, whose hatchet-wielding, Botox-pushing plastic surgeons have pulled them to the very edge of acceptable tightness, coming out of their Bentleys, Lamborghinis, and Porsches.

"This is lovely," says Mindy, inspecting the fancy-casual surroundings as she sits across from me. "I've never been here before."

"Really? With all the rich clients you have? This is shopping mecca for the Miamillionaires."

"Maddie, I don't meet with any other clients at chic restaurants to discuss their cases," she laughs. "I only do this for you. But this is definitely a pleasant way to conduct business."

"So let's get you a drink and make it even more pleasant. I can see the bottom of my glass, so I need a refill myself."

"No, no, I have to go back to the office right after lunch, and I have a rule about drinking during working hours," she says while she reviews the menu.

Our waiter appears with a basket of warm, superb, *my-nonna-loves-me*-style homemade Italian bread, and we order my wine and Mindy's lemon water.

"What'd you get?" She eyes the bag on the floor next to me.

"Oh, this? I was in desperate need of some essentials." Wink, wink.

"Essentials from Prada?" I detect a touch of judgment in her question.

"Yes, and after lunch I have to pick up some other essentials they're altering for me at Versace. Problem?"

My words hang heavily in the balmy air. Mindy's reaction to my snarky tone is her trademark inscrutable expression. The waiter returns with our drinks and distributes them on the table with theatrical flamboyance. "Are you lovely ladies ready to order?"

"Yes, I'll have a personal margherita pizza," I say, thankful that he has arrived to save me from my own impertinence. He turns to Mindy.

"Fettuccine Dolce Vita, thank you." She hands him the menu and, immediately after he withdraws, removes her leather-bound legal pad from a briefcase.

"Let me bring you up to speed on where we are. The child

support issue is a closed case. There was no balking on Richard's part there. Now, on the overall settlement, there are still some points of contention, but nothing that I can anticipate will be a problem."

"Do I get to keep the house? That's what keeps me up at night."

"That is one of the points we're discussing. There's a need for some negotiation, but quite frankly I would lose some respect for his attorney if he didn't huff and puff a little. It's all part of the drama. That is not at the top of the priority list. We'll get that coming or going. I'm putting more emphasis on studying his asset portfolio and making sure it's fully transparent. We have a team of forensic accountants at the ready in case we need to investigate the validity of his disclosed income statements. I'm sure Counselor Margolies knows I don't play."

"I just want to stay in my house. I don't want my kids to lose the home they love." The wine is having an effect, and I hear my words slur slightly. Every time I talk about all this, those infernal bees start buzzing in my ears again. Why does it all have to be so complicated?

"Maddie, trust me. There are several ways to address the house, but again, I want to be completely sure that we're getting a full picture of what he's bringing to the table."

"Do you think he could try to hide something?"

"Not if he and his attorney are smart. I've included a disclosure clause in the draft with language that requires all property be disclosed by both parties. It also states, *warns* if you read between the lines, that if a party does not reveal an asset, it may be subject to further discovery and future division as part of the marital property, as well as any additional legal fees. As of today, I haven't heard any objections."

"Well, it looks like you've done your due diligence and have all the angles covered. Mindy Johnson, Esquire, from the firm of Wasserman, Katz, Soto & Badass." I sigh with relief and allow myself an inordinately long sip of my wine.

"It's not my first rodeo," Mindy says with a tilt of her head and a half grin.

Our lunches arrive and after thanking the waiter, we dig in immediately. I realize I haven't had nourishment at all since I left the house this morning in delirious anger.

"So, what've you been doing with yourself these days?" Mindy asks me after savoring a few swirly forkfuls of her fettuccini, and the harsh edge of hunger has abated.

"Being a lady of leisure is not all it's cracked up to be. I'm tired of manis, pedis, and ladies' lunches. I'm restless. I'm thinking of renewing my nursing license anyway. Then I could really be of help at the community center."

"Fine, then. When the divorce is final, do it. Anything you achieve because you want to and not because you need to will give you more power and more freedom."

"It's not going to be easy. I have virtually no study habits left, plus my ADD is in the hi-def end of the spectrum, so that won't help."

"I hear ya. You just have to buck up, suck it up, and charge through it. This will be a very good thing for you. I'm proud of you."

Her words carry a long-forgotten yet familiar resonance that I can't quite place. Oh yes. I recognize it now. It's the faraway echo of true friendship.

Mindy

•

I manage to slip into my office virtually unnoticed after lunch with Maddie, but it's only a matter of time before the call comes for the compulsory yet pointless partners' meeting. I'm so over all of this. Nilda surreptitiously comes into my office and locks the door behind her to go over what my schedule holds for the afternoon. This gives me a moment to breathe and enjoy the tiny *colada* cup of liquid speed that Cubans call coffee, which she so intuitively knows I need.

As I expected, first on the agenda is more of Madeline Montiel's thorny dissolution. I think I was pretty straight with Maddie. On the very scant positive side, Montiel and his attorney seem to have been forthcoming during discovery, and I've been able to keep my claws retracted so far.

"Okay, hit me, what's going on?"

"Well, I think everything is *rrready* for the Montiel draft," she says in her deliciously thick, *r*-rolling Cuban accent.

"Mr. Montiel's attorney still hasn't voiced any objections to the disclosure clause?"

"*Bueno*, the last time he call he wasn't happy, you know? He say you sound like you think they hiding something."

"How did you respond?"

"I say, '*Ay no, Señor Margolies!* Miss Johnson always include this clause. Is *standar'*.'" She reenacts her conversation with the opposing counsel with all the dramatic flair of a Spanish TV *novela*.

"Well, you didn't exactly lie. I do think that little detail discourages people from trying to hide assets from the get-go. Nobody wants to go back to court after the divorce is final because someone got caught concealing goodies, least of all me. I doubt it's going to be a problem. I suspect Montiel wants to know what his 'exit fee' is going to be so he can move on with his new life. What else do we have on the docket?"

"You got another call from the Senator Rampling office on your private line." Here, her tone is dispirited as she looks at her long, fake, lollipop-red nails to avoid my gaze.

"Relax, Nilda, I haven't said yes yet."

"You haven't said no either." She pouts as she collects my empty *colada* cup and gently leaves my office.

To my surprise, I am touched by her concern at the prospect of my leaving the firm. I don't yield easily to displays of emotion, but Nilda and I have been together since I came to work at what then seemed a leviathan of a law office, fresh out of law school and green as I was regardless of my impeccable scholastic record.

On paper, attending Harvard Law School gave me the brightness of a supernova. In reality, it was just as cataclysmic. As my time in school quickly approached its end, I became more and more anxious about leaving the protective confines of academia. As long as I was a student, I didn't have to become a grown-up and make decisions about my future. My terror reached such a dangerous level that it took me three times to pass the bar, not for lack of knowledge but because of the impossibility of passing a test while staring at it for hours in a state of complete mental and physical paralysis.

The night after my second attempt, I took refuge in the coolness of my bathroom floor, flat on my back, in total darkness, fully aware that I had failed again. In the agonizing silence, as I stared fixedly in the direction of the invisible ceiling, I heard a voice from within softly pleading for guidance, or perhaps sanity, surrendering to whatever deity might listen. The voice that answered, although different from the first, also came from within. It said it didn't matter. I got it. I finally understood why I didn't feel the fire. It really didn't matter to me. My heart wasn't in it. So what if I never got to practice law? For a moment, I thought of chucking it all and finding a different direction. Lord knows I had enough credentials to find gainful employment. But I felt my dread morph into a sense of clarity, and I wondered if I would also now look at the exam through a different lens.

I told myself that the third attempt at passing the bar would simply be an experiment, that not one single life choice would be made based on the outcome. I took a job as a restaurant hostess, deliberately avoiding the predictable position at any law firm doing mindless research, filed the necessary paperwork to take the test again, and waited. I watched my fellow failed candidates feverishly study, review, discuss, and take prep classes. I didn't move a finger. Two months later, I passed the bar. Three weeks after that, Mr. Gerardo Soto asked me to join his illustrious law firm based solely on a glowing recommendation from my Family Court Litigation professor, no interview needed.

All the murkiness of those collegiate days had dissipated, but in its aftermath, some residual unsteadiness remained as I officially entered adulthood, and Nilda became my balance barre, my stability during those first unsure steps into the convoluted dance of divorce law. Now, after four short years, I am fatigued with the strife, the rancor, the devastation that accompanies all but a very few of the cases I handle.

That is not to say that I have trouble keeping a professional distance, but no one can be totally impervious to the ill will that often pervades the dissolution of a marriage, and I am ready to make a change and to *effect* some change. Maybe if I alter the blueprint of my professional life to one of service, my whole world will follow in the transformation. I cannot continue to work only to contribute to my bank account. I can do more. I want to do more, and when I got the scoop on an open position as a legislative assistant in the office of Senator Ted Rampling, member of the US Senate Committee on Environment and

Public Works, I began to wonder if Washington might be the setting for that change.

My impetus for making inquiries about the job came from two sources: my knowledge of the senator's work on environmental reform, and tenacious encouragement from one of a few wealthy, connected, influential people I've met during my time in the world of high-stakes divorce. Mrs. Dale Bates-Conway, one of my earliest clients, and one of the top five settlements I've ever secured, got a kick out of how clumsy and green I was, and instantly took a liking to me. Or felt sorry for me, I can't decide. But I was hungry to prove myself, and she enjoyed watching me fight for her through my tumbles and fumbles. Whenever our schedules permit, we steal some time to catch up, and she tells me how she's changing the world that day, and I tell her how I want to be just like her when I grow up.

Dale loves a project. She's not just a serious financial benefactor to many causes. She's hands-on. Most of her pictures in society pages don't show her decked out in jewels, but wearing a hard hat in the middle of a pile of rubble that will one day be a children's hospital or a homeless shelter. She's a mover, a shaker, and a trouble-maker in all the right ways and in the most powerful echelons of business and politics. And when she learned about the opportunity in Rampling's office, she convinced me to try for it with the promise of discretion and a good word in the Senator's ear, given my total inexperience in the political arena.

"Just try, see what happens," she said. "If it doesn't work out, fine. But you never know. Rampling needs some fresh blood in that office, and you are more than qualified for the job as I see it."

Her confidence is intoxicating, but I'm not ignorant of the fact that she contributed significant amounts of money to Rampling's reelection campaign, and financial supporters are priority stakeholders in the business of politics. Even so, I never really expected to be considered. Once again, though, my Harvard reputation, my performance in some high-profile cases involving other members of the senator's inner circle, and Dale's endorsement serving as the icing, caught his attention.

I stare at the phone message knowing that when I return the call, I will receive a pitch, yet another after about ten I've already heard from Rampling's office, describing what wonderful superhero deeds the senator has accomplished and how my professional life would be enriched by joining his team. They make it sound like Disney World.

At this point, I don't need to be sold on it. I am leaning heavily in the direction of accepting the position, but there are some variables for which I still need to account, and just as I begin to go down that short list, Nilda reappears at my door recovered from her melancholy, from the looks of the ample smile on her face. Behind her is the reason for the uplift in her mood.

My sister Ruby tries to walk over to kiss me hello, but an obstruction impedes her path. Little Hattie has just made a rush toward me worthy of a star running back, and leaps onto my lap with such force I know there will be bruises on my thighs later. She hugs me tight around the waist, and then she passionately closes her cherubic arms around my neck while placing her head on my shoulder. I peek down to see her little eyes closed.

"We made cookies today. Smushy chocolate chip."

"Yum! Did you save me some or did you eat them all?"

"I would never do that, Tía! And Mommy *hided* them from me anyway." The stinker. This is the only real item on that list of variables that keeps me in Miami.

"Tía Mimi, please, please say yes." She lifts her lips to my ear and whispers. It's almost a prayer.

"Yes—to—what?" I intersperse kisses between words as I savor her fleshy cinnamon cheeks. I hope she never learns to say *Mindy*, even when she's thirty-five. And I still can't get over the giggles that overcome me every time she calls me *tía*, a word she heard another four-year-old speak on the first day at her almost all Hispanic day care center. I watched awestruck as she tapped the little boy on the shoulder and said, "Excuse me, why do you call your mommy *tía*?" After a chortle, the boy explained the lady with him wasn't his mom but his aunt. From that day on, I was Tía Mimi.

"Tell her, Mommy." Now she opens her eyes to look at Ruby, and her tone is respectfully commanding.

Names and titles carry weight in our family. Ruby chose the name Hattie for no other reason than the fact that she read in a book of baby names that its Teutonic meaning was "home ruler." I believe as she carried her in her belly and faced the prospect of raising her as a single mother, she sensed that this child would have absolute sovereignty over anyone living under her roof. It became a self-fulfilling prophecy. Hattie is the hub where all our lives converge. She is the only sun that brightens Ruby's days, she holds our mother's heart hostage, she is our younger and wilder sister Nadine's reality check, and for me she represents the one and only outlet for expressing love, unabated and unconditional. Without her my connection to humanity would be precariously limited, I'm afraid.

"Hattie has been crossing out days on the calendar and has come to the sudden realization that the summer is flying by and we haven't taken a trip." Ruby perches herself on the arm of the sofa in my office. "Since she's been on a princess kick, I thought I'd take her to Magic Kingdom, but she doesn't want to go without you. She says you're a better princess than I am."

She shrugs and gives me a half smile. I know my sister feels blessed that we are such a tight-knit family, but I sometimes sense a subtle hint of jealousy where Hattie and I are concerned. It is a remarkable relationship. Even to others in the family it seems that Ruby was my surrogate and I the mother. But perhaps we wouldn't be so close if I were her mother.

"Look Tía Mimi, there's only a little bit of days left." She proceeds to take out a carefully folded copy of a calendar from the glittery pink saddle bag she's so stylishly wearing cross-body over her lavender sundress. I try to replicate the grave expression with which she is presenting her case as I survey the calendar in front of me, and I notice, to my dismay, that indeed more than half the summer has already been crossed out in purple crayon. Between the Montiel case, the community center fund-raiser looming ahead, and my indecisiveness about the job in Washington, the summer is quickly evaporating in the humid Miami sun.

"I told her you're too busy right now and that Nadine, Mom, and I would take her, but she's a stubborn little thing, isn't she?" It appears that Ruby has been making her own strong case for asserting her maternal position. A conundrum: It would be good for Hattie to get used to not having me around all the time and strengthening her bond with her mother. That said, the idea of saying *no* seems the darkest of cruelties, not just for the child but for myself as well. Not to mention that if I do take the DC job, I need to clock as much time as possible with my pixie.

To comply with this unexpected request, which, let's face it, I have already decided I will, I would have to leave some loose ends, like the Montiel case and the fund-raiser, and somehow squeeze in a trip to Washington for a meeting with the senator. Tall order indeed. My four-year-old niece has just schooled me on the fact that this is the time for action, the time to abandon my lassitude.

"So what are we going to do on our mini-vacation?"

Hattie's face lights up like a thousand suns, yet I notice a furtive wave of disappointment cross my sister's face.

"We're going to be princesses!" Apparently, this is a given because Hattie looks at me as if she's just stated something that should be obvious. I may be headed for Capitol Hill, but this little elf is not impressed. "And … we both have to keep our tiaras on all the time like princesses have to do," she says, pointing a warning finger at me, lest I dare consider not meeting her terms.

"So I guess then we have to marry a prince?" I'm fully committed to this now.

And then the wisdom of the ages pours forth from this tiny sage. She cups my face in her little hands and in the most innocently lofty tone educates me again. "Oh, Tía Mimi, you don't need a prince to be a princess."

From the mouths of babes.

••

The clouds are dense, the sky is the color of cement, and the humidity comes with built-in skin adhesive even at six thirty in the morning. A feeble drizzle struggles to make itself noticed. Merely two days after Hattie's royal command for a Disney vacation, Ruby is driving me to the airport, and the ride has been silent so far. I am lost in the recurring memory of my early good-bye with Hattie. It was selfish of me to wake her at such an ungodly hour just to hug and kiss her before I left, but the heart wants what the heart wants. I have allowed myself to justify the dreadful act with the idea that she would've been upset if I'd left furtively under cover of dark dawn. Besides, it took a total of thirty seconds. But I know it's the guilt I feel for entertaining the possibility of a more permanent goodbye. I peeled the covers off her, took her soft, warm little body in my arms, kissed her forehead, and when she opened her big brown doe eyes, I simply whispered, "I'll be home tonight. I love you."

She smiled, pressed herself closer to me, and locked her half-shut eyes with mine in a look that I interpreted to say please be safe, I'll miss you, and how could you even consider a move somewhere far away when you know I can't live without you? All she said, though, was a sleepy "Love you, Tía Mimi."

"Are you nervous?" Ruby interrupts my contemplation.

"I wouldn't call it nervous. I'm anxious to take a good look at the offer and the job description so I can make a decision. I'm surprised they've waited for me this long."

"But you must have some idea of whether the job suits you, and I know you wouldn't be taking this trip if you didn't think it was worth it. This could be long-term, you know? You could be set for life."

I know where she's going with this, and I'm getting exasperated. "Okay, Ruby, stop. Yes, it's a great opportunity, yes, I need to think about my future, and no, I'm still not sure I want to take the job. Back off, please." I knew she was feeling a little possessive about Hattie, but this is starting to sound like an all-out campaign to get me far away from her.

No other words are spoken until she drops me off at the terminal and we say our good-byes.

The reluctant drizzle in Miami turns to sheets of driving rain in DC that force the pilot to keep us in a holding pattern for twenty minutes. Rather than give in to impatience, I turn my thoughts away from the delay and the impending meeting. I make a mental list of things I want to do with Hattie on our vacation. I wonder which princess costume she'll want to add to her collection this time. I'm betting on Jasmine. She's been driving her mother crazy lately with her new crop top obsession so she can show her plump baby midriff. And we'll have to stay at a Disney-themed hotel. The last time we were there she was only two and didn't have such defined plans for immersion into her favorite fairy-tale fantasies.

These are the thoughts floating around in my head when the tower finally clears us for landing. I'm glad the senator insisted on sending a car to pick me up. I do so like the special treatment, no secret there.

This isn't the first time I've been to Washington, but today I feel a sense of ownership while an ultra-preppy page leads me through the splendid halls of the Russell Senate Office Building, located a stone's throw from the grand Capitol. As I catch a glimpse of the iconic dome through a stretch of windows, I could swear the soul of the structure welcomes me. Who can resist the romanticism of it all?

Owen Benjamin, the legislative director and my prospective immediate superior in the chain of command, and a tall, Olive Oyl-thin woman whose severe spinster fashion style seems inconsistent with her young age, walk into the office where I sit. She introduces me, and when he offers me his hand with a firm shake, she quickly exits and closes the door behind her.

"Good afternoon, Miss Johnson, Owen Benjamin. Glad to finally meet 'ya. Heard a lot about you from the senator."

Ample, rapacious smile, with seemingly more teeth than the average human.

"He'll be meeting with you this afternoon as scheduled, but I thought you and I should talk about some general details regarding your responsibilities, should you take the position."

I wonder if I'll need to talk at all. He seems to have this under control.

"Tell me what you think I should know about you … Mindy, is it? Do you mind if I call you Mindy? Please call me Owen."

How can I call you anything when I haven't even said "Howdy"? "Sure, Mindy's fine. Well, other than what's in my résumé, there isn't anything else of consequence that I can say about myself. I spend the better part of my life working, so there really isn't much more to add." In other words, I have no life.

"Okay, well, are there any questions that I can answer for you?"

Come to think of it, I didn't prepare any questions. I thought these people were so eager to have me that I just came ready to hear another sales pitch. I'll wing it.

"Realistically, how hands-on would the position allow me to be? I mean, will I have the opportunity to communicate with constituents right out of the gate? That's important to me. Or will it center mostly on legal work?" That sounded pretty good, right?

"You're coming in with an advantage, Mindy. Senator Rampling seems to have an outline of how he wants to use you." His lips widen and he shows me more teeth than his chuckle requires. "Some of us had to prove ourselves." Bigger chuckle, even more teeth, somewhat acerbic tone.

Uh oh. I sense a disturbance in the Force.

•••

Senator Rampling's office is clearly an extension of his pontifical persona. While the room is not particularly spacious, the elegantly masculine décor makes it opulent and foreboding. Rampling sits nobly in his oversized, button-tufted, oxblood leather chair. Against one of the endlessly shelved walls, between the door and the desk, is an antique Victorian couch upholstered in a lush combination of printed velvet and brocade in shades of burnt orange and dark red.

The centerpiece of the space is the solid oak desk, which was evidently designed to intimidate. The top is covered with antiqued brown leather and rests on two massive pedestals dramatically detailed with Victorian carving. It faces the door squarely, and behind it, framing the senator's magisterial outline, a tall, narrow window with rich drapery matching the color of the chair almost to perfection provides a postcard view of Capitol Hill in the cloudy afternoon sky.

"As my legislative assistant, Miss Johnson, I expect you will become much more of an advisor to me than just an administrative processor. There's a set of community as well as global issues for which I would like you to be responsible. You will be tracking all legislation related to these issues, and I will expect you to advise me on the best way to address them or present them to the committee."

Senator Ted Rampling was probably a major player in his youth. Even in his sixties, he gives off an exotic scent of power and charisma well mixed together. He's not a particularly handsome man. In fact, he has an inordinately large forehead accentuated by his almost nonexistent hairline; his features are roundish and his lips too full for a man. He is, however, over six feet tall, with a vigorous frame, and wears his tailored suit impeccably. He speaks with a hypnotizing Southern drawl that makes his booming voice sound melodious.

"My intention is to keep you away from the more mundane functions. I want you to be my eyes and ears, Miss Johnson." Does he mean *spy*?

"I see you in the role of my representative to outside organizations, lobbyists, and advocacy groups with an interest in environmental legislation before Congress. You will be the face of this office." He flashes me a bright grin reminiscent of Owen Benjamin's, but somehow the senator's doesn't come off as shifty.

"With a little experience under your belt, I don't doubt you will have the opportunity to assume even greater responsibility as a legislative director."

"Is Mr. Benjamin looking to make a move?"

He leans in, plants his elbows on the colossal desk, and entwines his fingers as if ready to break into prayer. "Miss Johnson, I don't want to sound self-important, but an assignment in this office is quite a coveted position. We do good work here and a few political careers have taken off from this launching pad. Those who are privileged to work for me will gladly make whatever moves I require."

I feel a slight chill all over. I don't have a Pollyanna view of how Washington works by any means, but at this moment I realize that cunning has a certain tonality, and a musky fragrance, and a look of its own.

I notice that I have been holding my breath and it's caught in my throat. I want to swallow hard, but I don't want to give off the scent of fear. Luckily, the senator relaxes his body and leans back in his chair, the grin flashing brightly once again.

"Now tell me, Miss Johnson, what can I do to make your days here a professionally fulfilling experience? How do we seal this deal?"

"I'm hoping to assist you in helping constituents cut through red tape. I believe that would be a most rewarding part of the job." I say it almost like a question. "I feel that many times the community doesn't know who to turn to, and when a live person reaches out to them, they are appreciative and cooperative."

"Well, Miss Johnson, I can certainly allow you to do some of that if it gives you a sense of altruistic accomplishment, but I have a feeling that after a few months here, you'll want to get your hands a little dirtier." He chortles haughtily.

Up to now, I've been trying to stay in my place, be observant, and take everything at face value, but my discomfort at not fully grasping this man's meaning is growing by the second. Maybe I'm imagining things. I get the impression that everything he says has a double meaning, and I need a coin to decide how to interpret his words. Heads means he sees great potential in me and wants me to do great things within the legislative branch of our government. Tails means … Well, I won't worry right now about what tails could mean.

The rain has finally relented, and the skies are Titian blue outside my airplane window. A quiet stillness washes over me, and though I'm relieved that it's over, details of the meeting replay in the filmstrip of my mind. The entire episode lasted maybe two hours, and when it ended, I didn't have much more information about the job than when it started. There was some rhetoric, some political mixed metaphors, a bit of pep-talking, and a *very nice to meet you, Miss Johnson. Let us know what you decide and off you go.* How do they do that? Where do politicians learn to string together just the right words and manage to say nothing?

If I were to make a pros and cons list based on what I learned today, it might look like this. Pros: I might have the opportunity to become the intermediary between the senator's office and the constituents; I'd be on Capitol Hill; I'd be working on environmental and public issues (I think). Cons: I might not have the opportunity even to talk to constituents (Rampling didn't make any promises); I'd be far away in Washington; I might be asked to do some things that could bump against ethical boundaries, even working on environmental and public issues. I'm obsessing and obsessing requires energy that I don't have right now.

I am grateful for the smooth ride, and the steady drone of the engines lulls me into gentle drowsiness. I'm done. I'm taking off my thinking cap, and I'm putting on my tiara.

Sylvia

•

"If you think about it, *Star Trek* is a microcosm of all that humanity endures."

"Really? How so?" Inside my head I'm screaming *WHO THE HELL CARES?*

"It's problem-solving at its best, babe. Racism, anarchy, oppression, psychological instability, war, genocide—it's all there, and it challenges man to search for answers even when it seems no answer can be found. It forces them to go to the most unlikely places for those answers, you feel me? Where no man has gone before, babe." He winks and I flinch.

"I wasn't sure about coming to this here shindig, but you're a pretty rad chic, and this paint-while-you-sip deal is, like, pretty happening, don't you think?"

"Yeah … bitchin'."

The fact is I wasn't too sure about coming either, but an uneasiness has settled inside me, and I'm scared of standing still and letting it overtake me. Before now there was no question that I had no time or desire for social interaction with men, but now I feel ambivalent about wanting to open myself to dating. I blame Tony Clifton for that.

His constant and fruitless suggestions that we should get together for coffee, or drinks, or dinner, a gallery walk, an alligator rodeo in the Everglades, anything he can come up with, have gone from annoying to disturbing. His doggedness is getting harder to ignore.

It occurred to me that of all the choices offered by Synergy, an event called Bottle & Brush, involving wine and art, would be the most civilized and hopefully attract colorful yet sophisticated singles. Wrong! So far since I came into this large industrial basement, all I've seen is a few septuagenarians and this hippie retiree from Starfleet. Sparse strands of grizzled hair grow from the middle of his otherwise bald and freckled head and reach his shoulders. His tie-dyed T-shirt rises above his navel, but the waistband of his ripped jeans doesn't reach it. And this ensemble is accessorized by a lanyard on his wrist to complement his Medic Alert bracelet. Ugh! Beam me up.

A thirtysomething woman wearing a peasant skirt, a fringed vest, and espadrilles takes center stage. "Good evening everyone, and welcome to Bottle & Brush by Synergy. My name is Mariah and I will be your hostess this evening." She smiles broadly and gestures with her arms for all present to gather around her.

At this point, a few more people have joined, and I notice with relief that none seem to be old enough for the nursing home.

"We are very excited to have you and we promise that you will enjoy yourselves tremendously. You will each choose an easel, but please feel free to mingle. That is why we're here, right?" She extends her arms, chortles pretentiously, and begins clapping and urging us to join in the applause.

"Our servers will walk about with the different selections of wines, and there are hors d'oeuvres on the tables on each side of the room." She gestures to the tables like a flight attendant showing emergency exits on a plane.

The crowd has now swelled to about fifteen with a slight majority of females. Captain Kirk is distracted talking to Mariah, and I take the opportunity to walk to one of the food tables, and hopefully find an easel in a galaxy far away from him.

Up to now the most exciting prospect is the parade of wine trays they promised. I pile morsels of food into a pyramid on my tiny plate and hope to disappear into a corner to gorge myself.

I notice a tall man with an empty plate carefully surveying the snack choices as he slowly walks the length of the table. As he approaches, I discover he's not outright ugly, and I guess I've been staring too long because he suddenly looks up at me and smiles pleasantly. "Pretty good spread, huh?"

I feel warmth in my cheeks. "Yes, not bad. And the wine selection is decent too."

"Oh, it's always a treat to meet a fellow wine enthusiast." He lays his plate on the table and offers me his hand. "Eric Stewart."

"Sylvia Sabatino. It's a pleasure."

"So what do you do, Sylvia?"

"I'm in publishing, how about you?" Better not give too many details too soon.

"I'm an architect, mostly commercial."

Hmm, so far so good. By now we have settled in a cozy cove in the back of the room where only our two easels fit, and we have a panoramic view of the entire room. I notice Captain Kirk giving me a quick glare before turning his attention to a short, stout woman with hair shaped into a geometric bob that reminds me of Russian nesting dolls.

A white screen displaying a photograph of what looks like a Tuscan vineyard has now taken Mariah's place at the front of the room. She stands to the side of the screen and swivels around as she speaks, attempting to make eye contact with all present. I think she's giving tips for reproducing the image on our respective empty canvases and saying something about shading or shadows and pointillism, but I'm distracted by Eric's fixed gaze on something to his left. I lean slightly to see what has captured his attention, but all that stands beyond his stool is an emergency exit dimly lit by a naked yellowish lightbulb about ten steps away.

"Are you okay?" I tentatively place my hand on his arm.

He seems to return from his trance, empties his wineglass in one broad swig, and smiles. "Oh yes, I'm sorry. It's so dark by that door I almost didn't see him there."

I lean again and see nothing. "See who?"

"The old man, over there, right by the exit sign." He points to a faded sign by the door.

"I don't see anyone."

"He's gone now," he says almost to no one. "Please forgive me, I didn't mean to be rude. It's just that when it happens, I can't take my eyes off them."

Instantly, I'm overwhelmed with regret and I'm not even sure why. "When what happens?" I recoil in expectation of the answer.

Now he shifts to face me, and he looks squarely at me without blinking. "You see, Sylvia, I've been given a gift. I can see dead people."

Check, please!

••

Ponce de Leon Boulevard is a streaking blur through my car window. I am purple with rage at myself. I knew I shouldn't have gone to that horrific singles nightmare. I wasn't even expecting to meet anyone when I decided to try it. I did it because I wanted to shake things up, to see if any part of the adventurous, irrepressible Sylvia still existed. You would think the cosmos would cooperate and provide an encouraging experience, but after an evening with the Not So Good, the Bad, and the Maniacal, I just want to crawl into a ball and burrow under the covers. Why am I the only one who thinks I'm fine without a man? These are the moments when I have to fight the urge to call on my friends Ben and Jerry, and even miss my college boyfriends Jack Daniels and Johnny Walker.

A lackluster covering of clouds stretches over the late evening sky. My windshield wipers mix a misty drizzle with the dust on the glass into a pasty mud. Streetlights and building lights burn a hazy gold. Through the hot, angry tears in my eyes, headlights and taillights glow in ghostly halos. I want so much to hurt each one of those horrid girls and spit profanities at them for putting me in this position. I beat my steering wheel violently, an empty gesture since the wheel is infuriatingly unmoved. My first target could be Jo, only because I just drove past the hotel where she works. She wouldn't be there now anyway, I rationalize. At a red light, my eyes shift and I do a double take. Isn't that her coming out of O'Malley's Tavern? And who is she with? Is that … *Tony Clifton*? No, it can't be. What would those two be doing together? And why wouldn't Jo tell me?

Hmm … strange. I'm having a hard time coming up with a reason for this coupling. More importantly, though, why am I feeling betrayed? My breathing is short, I'm lightheaded, and I feel a crater in the pit of my stomach. Why do I suddenly wish I had a weapon in my purse more threatening than a pair of tweezers? Ah! What do I care what they do? But I do care.

For the first time in ages, I don't want to go into the office. It took immense effort to simmer down long enough to doze into a broken sleep fraught with disjointed images of wine glasses floating in space and moving paintings of ghosts haunting a bucolic landscape where Jo and Tony frolic happily, all the while laughing at me. I think this isn't supposed to hurt, but it does.

I wish I hadn't told my friends and Minerva that I was going to that infernal matchmaking loony bin. If I tell them what treasures I found, they will think it uproarious. I don't find it funny. Is that what the dating scene is like these days? I shudder to think.

Plus, the cherry on top. As if my wasted evening hadn't been enough, I'm disturbingly uneasy about seeing Jo and Tony together. Edit that. I'm having paroxysms of jealousy. Is it because perhaps he's turning his attention to more productive endeavors, seeing as I've turned him down so many times? Why did the persistent memory of my friend and that man burn me with rage all night? I resolve to forget about it by focused willpower, but the more I concentrate on forgetting, the more I think about it, and the more I think about it, the more enraged I become, and the more enraged I become, the more I think about it! Madness.

"Minnie, I'm going to review the layouts and make some phone calls from home. I woke up with a migraine and I took some pills, so I don't want to drive just now."

Mentioning the horse pills will make this phone call brief. "Is there anything pressing I need to know about?"

"Nope. I'll email you the headshots we got yesterday from Chic Models. If you see any you like, we can get the contracts ready. Also, Tony Clifton called to say the rough cut of your interview is ready if you want to see it. Should I have him send it here?"

The mention of his name sends a prickly wave down my spine. "Uh, no … I'll take care of it."

I lean back in my office chair and stare at the phone for minutes after I hang up. There's a tug-of-war going on inside me: One part of me is revved up and eager to spring into action as the desperate beginnings of a plan to investigate the Jo-Tony alliance form in my mind. Another part of me holds me hostage and rigidly gripped by this chair. I sense that the first option, to dig for details, may reveal truths that could change my life in yet inexplicable and frightening ways. The other option, to do nothing, will take me deeper into isolation with only newfound bitterness as a travel companion.

•••

There's a half-eaten Twinkie on Tony Clifton's desk in the office he's borrowing from the network affiliate while on assignment. He's wearing jeans and an untucked, long-sleeved, perfectly crisp white shirt that matches his perfectly wide, contagious smile. Damn.

"I appreciate you taking the time to come. The piece turned out great and I thought we could watch it together, and you can tell me if there's anything you'd like to change."

"Not a problem. My day has been light."

"Ahh, come on, confess. You took the day off just to come see me," he says in a silky voice.

Here we go again. Can't this man ever take anything seriously? Narcissist.

"Go on, laugh a little. It improves your appetite for passion."

Now he's stretching. Besides, you can't improve on something that's dead.

"Perhaps there's a woman somewhere who will relish the opportunity to share a laugh with you. I'll pass."

"You're the only woman in my life right now." He grins with a wink.

Save your little wink, thank you very much.

"I am not *any* woman in your life. Besides, you're not the type of man to have only one woman in your life at a time, are you?" I begin to probe for answers.

"Ouch! That stings. I'll tell you what. You don't ask me about my dating habits, and I won't ask you your age. At least not until after our first official date." He leans back and laughs.

"Funny. I didn't know you were originally from Never Never Land."

"See? That wasn't so hard, was it? A bit of levity is always a good thing."

One person's levity is another's biting sarcasm. This punk tugs at my sanity. I just met him a virtual minute and a half ago, and he has a road map to all my push-buttons. His presence gives me the creeps. He chafes my nerves raw. And his arrogance. And his twinkly wink. And that stupid, luminescent smile. There's an uncomfortable and unfamiliar alchemy between us. My foot is tapping involuntarily again. It seems to happen every time I'm around this guy. Tony Clifton gives me a nervous tic.

I'm suddenly aware of how rigidly I cling to my chair, and it seems Tony has also noticed my immense discomfort. He leans against the front of his desk, crosses his ankles and arms, tilts his head, and giggles a little.

"What are you going to do without me when I leave next week?"

Next week? Next week! I'm unable to utter a word for fear I will reveal my anguish.

"Geez, I can see you're heartbroken over the news," he says with a little misery in his voice and returns to his chair. Clearly, he has mistaken my silence for indifference. Good.

"Sylvia, I'm a big screwup, I'll be the first one to admit it, but I have learned one thing about life. Having a high IQ, as obviously you do, does not necessarily mean that you're able to distinguish friend from foe. I promise you, my intentions have always been friendly."

"Are you selling dime-store wisdom?"

"No, but you should find someone who is, 'cause you need to stock up." He reaches for his phone to answer the buzzing intercom. "Yep, let her in."

Before I can even process the rudeness of his last comment, I am bulldozed by the sight of Jo walking into the office. She greets both of us with warm kisses and hellos, sits next to me, and squeezes my hand warmly.

"Thanks so much for inviting me, Tony. I am so excited about watching this interview. I love to hear Sylvia talk passionately about her work."

"You are most welcome. I thought it would be a nice surprise for Sylvia, and you get to see some of my work."

"Are you surprised? You would've never guessed that I'd be here, huh?" She turns to me.

"I'll say. What is surprising is that you would leave your kitchen to come here in the middle of a workday. Clifton must be very persuasive." I am positive that my unease is evident because I'm not making any great effort to disguise it.

"He can be very convincing, no doubt about that." Jo and Tony give each other a look of tacit understanding that infuriates me. "But I thought the three of us could go out for lunch after we watch the piece. My treat. I got connections in the restaurant world, you know?"

Don't do me any favors.

"Lunch with the two most interesting women in Miami. Gosh, I love my job!" Tony rubs his hands together and ends with a clap of delight.

"Just don't let me drink more than one glass of wine. I think I overdid it last night."

"Nah! Nonsense! You were enchanting."

And there it is. A blatant admission of guilt. I look at Jo quizzically and she reads the question in my head clearly.

"Tony and I had drinks last night at O'Malley's."

"I see. What was the occasion, if I'm allowed to ask?" Even I can hear the disdain in my tone.

"I stopped at the hotel for dinner, and I had to buy the chef a drink to thank her for the spectacular dessert." He gushes at Jo and kisses her hand. I feel a rocket lighting up under me and about to launch me off the chair.

Presumably in an attempt to appease me, she searches my gaze and smiles. "We talked about you and the piece almost the entire time. That's why he called me right after you said you were coming today. You know I'm your biggest fan, Sylvia. I got your back, girl."

"I believe you," I offer without reciprocating the smile. *Right, and I believe in the tooth fairy too.* "But I think I'd like to reschedule our meeting, Mr. Clifton. I feel our focus on the piece has been compromised, and I have no time for socializing and leisurely lunches on a workday. You two enjoy, by all means." My speech is broken, and my words erupt from my lips fueled by the resentment boiling inside me. I rise from the chair and fight the urge to bolt out the door.

"Wait … what …" Jo struggles to begin her sentence. I take advantage of the fact that they are both stunned and see my way out. Take that, *friends*.

••••

Belgian chocolates, shortbread cookies, gelato, wine, artisan crackers, hummus, Nutella, wine, a big wedge of stinky, expensive French cheese, prosciutto, wine… How many bottles of wine was that? Who cares! My mouth waters as I watch my purchases slide down the conveyor toward the Whole Foods cash register. The clerk has an excited expression on her face every time she scans an item. You'd think she works on commission.

There was a time when I would've called the foodie group and met them at some fabulous eatery for some venting. Inevitably, more than one member of the group besides me would confess to needing a night out to unload whatever drama they were presently enduring. Today, that would not work. Today, I want to hole up in my apartment and stuff myself. I don't think I've binged like this since college. To hell with watching my weight, to hell with my cholesterol, to hell with all my so-called friends.

Someday I'll be sad, but right now I'm angry. Mostly at myself for taking a peek out of my shell just to be slammed back into it. To think for a second I actually thought of seducing him right there in his office. The horror! One day, I'll stumble upon the long-forgotten interview with Tony, and my eyes will burn with tears. I'll remember the moment when hope foolishly reappeared in my heart, and the pain of that memory will make the emptiness inside sting for just an instant. But right now, I'm angry, and the sadness will be drowned in all these legal substances smiling at me from the shopping cart.

I drive impatiently to my building, trudge to my elevator, trying to juggle way too many grocery bags, and Alex, one of the two front desk security guards, quickly jumps to my aid. He takes the bags and gives me a fat manila envelope in return.

"Good afternoon, Ms. Sabatino. This came from your office a few hours ago." I dump it into my briefcase without even looking at it. Nothing outside of these brown bags holds any interest for me right now.

After thanking Alex for helping me carry the treasures into my cave and promptly dismissing him, I meticulously distribute every item between tables and other surfaces, almost the same way I organize magazine layouts in my conference room. I slip into pajamas and a robe, close the blinds until the room is as dark as my eyes can tolerate, and immediately turn my attention to the first bottle of wine. I've never liked drinking alone, so I turn on the TV and surf through the channels mindlessly, fascinated by the amount of drivel airing during the afternoon hours of a weekday. I find a rerun of *America's Next Top Model*, and I raise my glass at Tyra Banks, who seems to be angry at one of the contestants. They both look like they need some of this wine.

I'm fighting the urge to go into business mode and assess the models on the screen, so I distract myself by piling globs of Nutella over two shortbread cookies and gluing them together into a sandwich. But business mode is my safe place. It's the mindset that gives me control over my world. Maybe that will be my next venture—a modeling agency. And all the models would be size twelve and above. No stick figures in my agency. The concept of beauty is in a revolution. With my experience, I could definitely put my stamp on that field.

I'm digging my way through a mine of chocolate bits in my pint of *stracciatella* gelato and rinsing it with wine when my cell phone chirps. It's my office. When I don't answer, a text from Minnie comes in almost immediately. Interrupting a scorned woman halfway through a pint of gelato is never a safe thing to do, everybody knows that. The office building could be invaded by zombies and I wouldn't care right now. The problem is Minerva won't give up if it's important. Four minutes later, the phone rings again.

"Talk." This is my way of warning her to make it short.

"Problem. The Thailand shoot is a bust. Some typhoon skirted the coast, and by the time the crew could go outside again, they only had a day left, and there was nothing but torn-up stilt houses and flooded streets. Most of the pictures they managed to take look dreary and cloudy. Didn't you get the proofs I sent?" She ends with a deep intake of breath.

I remove the envelope from my briefcase and notice the word "URGENT" in big red block letters. I toss it aside and ignore the question.

"We have to either do it again or pick another venue," I say as clearly as I can through a mouthful of hummus and cracker.

"We may not make the deadline and the travel feature may have to be cut from the issue. Also, Andreas wants double his fee if he has to fly over there again or he won't do it."

Now that I didn't need to hear. It's been a long time since a freelancer tried to strong-arm me. Today is the wrong day to try. I have a few options: I can call this bonehead photographer and take out all my frustrations on him, which would definitely deter him from ever putting conditions on me again. That would just make me look unattractively rabid. I could simply fire him. That wouldn't give me as much satisfaction. I could just do the job myself. Just fly to Thailand and disappear for a while. No, it's too humid over there. My hair would turn to straw and I'd look like a scarecrow. I think the calorie rush is making me delirious.

I rip a chunk of cheese too big for one bite, wrap it in a slice of prosciutto, and stuff it into my mouth. It's hard to chew and breathe, but I can't stop. I refuse to stop.

The ominous rumbling in my stomach tells me that I'm traveling at the speed of light toward gastrointestinal damnation, and yet I have another cheese-and-prosciutto bomb at the ready. Self-destruction is addictive.

Suddenly, I'm assaulted by a cacophony of sounds. My stomach sounds and feels like a cement mixer, Minerva's voice has gone up an octave as she rambles on about the consequences of this latest crisis, troubleshooting options swirl around in my head like a twister, and now the doorbell is ringing. I suppose it's either someone from maintenance or Alex from the front desk, so if I ignore it, they will respectfully retreat.

I quickly dismiss Minnie with assurances that I will magically fix everything. Now there's banging mixed in with the doorbell. Who *is* that?

Josephine

•

"Sylvia, open this door!" I press my ear to the gap between the double doors to the penthouse and I can hear her scurrying around.

"I know you're in there, I can hear you, so open this damn door!" I yell into the gap as I ring the bell repeatedly and mix it up with knocking … no, banging, on the door.

"Go away!"

Finally. "I'm not going anywhere. I'll have this conversation from out here if I have to, and already two of your neighbors have given me angry looks." Nothing.

"Sylvia, I don't know how much of my Brooklyn ghetto ways the people who live in this uppity building are going to tolerate, so get ova' yourself and open up!" Words I accentuate with another bang on the Greek-trimmed, pristine white door.

Just as I'm about to pound again, the door opens violently and the breeze lifts Sylvia's white satin robe behind her in a flourish. Very dramatic. She faces me, her eyes shrunken to slits with ferocity, and holds the handle with clear intent to slam the door as soon as I speak or attempt to enter.

She doesn't scare me—much. I walk past her in slow motion without taking my eyes off her. She holds my gaze. Two lionesses ready to pounce. She closes the door in a controlled, deliberate move and places her hands on her hips.

"What do you want? And why didn't the front desk tell me you were here?" She spews the words.

"I spend as much time here as I do in my own place. The front desk guys know me, and I told them you were expecting me. What the hell's the matter with you? What's with the psychotic tantrum in Tony's office?" I say, as I plop on her couch. I try to put my purse on her vast sea-green velvet tufted ottoman coffee table, but there isn't one inch that isn't covered with food, food wrappers, and bottles of wine. A binge equals emotional upheaval in Sylvia's world. I know I shouldn't be so harsh with her, but I can't help it. She behaved like a child today.

"Forgive me, but when people are trying to make a fool of me, I don't usually stick around. And get off my couch!"

"What are you talking about? I thought we were all having a pleasant visit, although come to think of it, you didn't look too thrilled when I showed up," I say, ignoring her demand to stand.

"Why *did* you show up? You drop in on him out of the blue with frequency?"

"I have once or twice since you introduced us. I told you, I like him. He's a nice man and very good company. What do you care what I'm doing with Tony, anyway? You chew him up and spit him out on a daily basis."

"The point is I had a business meeting with him, and when you came it all changed. The two of you were throwing teases and witticisms at each other and reminiscing about your little rendezvous. Suddenly I felt like the third wheel. *And I was there first!*" she yells over the persistent ringing of my cell phone, which I have ignored for the past few seconds.

"You're insane. He talks like that to everyone. He was even playful and charming with you, but you were too busy readjusting the stick up your butt to play along!" I can't take it any longer and I pull the phone from my bag and answer without identifying the caller.

"Yes?" I snap. I'm mortified that I've allowed Sylvia to agitate me.

"Hey! What's going on? You both left like the place was on fire."

Tony. Well, this is it. Go big or go home. I haven't decided whether I will tell Sylvia tonight the nature of my relationship with Tony, but I'm going to try my best to make her admit to herself that she wants him. This might hurt a bit, but it's for her own good. Not to mention she might hurt me—physically, but I'm willing to take that chance.

"Hi, Tony, yeah ... I'm sorry. That was quite a good-bye, huh?" I chuckle a little.

Sylvia is ready to spit nails again.

"Is everything okay?" he asks, concerned.

"Yes, yes, please don't worry. Everything is—will be fine, I assure you." Who's going to assure me?

Sylvia glides over to me and whispers violently in my ear, "Everything is not fine."

"You sound different, Jo. Are you with Sylvia right now?" The realization shocks him.

"Uh … yes, that would be lovely."

"Okay. I get it. I'll play along. Call me when you can." He's gone.

In a bold move, I throw my head back and laugh heartily. "Tony, you just don't give up, do you? Okay, you win. I'll see you tomorrow night." I hang up and return the phone to my bag, still smiling. At least if she kills me, he'll know where to send the cops to find my body.

Immediately she lunges forward with an accusing finger pointed at me. "You see? That's it, right there! There's something going on with you two, don't deny it!"

"Define 'something.'"

"Don't play with me, Jo. Spill it."

"If you're asking me whether we are romantic, the answer is it's none of your business. However, for the sake of our friendship, I will say this: He hasn't made any inappropriate moves, and contrary to what you may believe, I have no designs on him—yet."

She breathes deeply and her features soften somewhat with relief.

"Thank you. I hope you understand that it's very uncomfortable for me to work with him thinking that you're involved in some way," she says sounding a bit self-satisfied. I don't know that I like that.

"So, what's the deal? You don't want him but no one else can have him either?" Now *I'm* a little inflamed. "I've had enough of this, Sylvia. The jig is up. You listen here, I got news for you. Not everyone in your life has to tolerate being treated like one of your minions. I'm not on the payroll." As I deliver my tirade, I've forced her to take at least three steps back.

"I'm going to say this only once. I have no romantic interest in Tony at all. But you like this man; you like him a lot, and now it just might be too late. I get that you're scared witless of this reality, but you should've reevaluated your manufactured opinion of him a long time ago, put on your big-girl panties, or better even, you should've let *him* take them off!" The force and content of these last words thrust her into the couch. She closes her open mouth, lowers her gaze, defeated, and pulls at the hair on her temples.

"Well?" I have no patience left.

"I'm thinking, I'm thinking," she says as she scoops a precariously large amount of hummus with a cracker and shoves it nervously in her mouth. "Okay, maybe all the flirting did wear me down," she manages to say while she chews the enormous mouthful. "It just didn't occur to me that he could be spreading it around, or that he might get tired of trying. Maybe I *am* attracted to him and maybe I didn't realize it because every time I'm around him, my stomach swims in nausea."

I feel sorry for her at this moment. Her face displays a pitiful combination of humility, despondency, and disgust with herself. Mission accomplished. She's finally facing her feelings. "Well, you did this to yourself. Leave me out of it. And you know, love feels a lot like nausea." For a moment I entertain the thought of telling her why Tony and I have been meeting, but I'm so hurt by her mistrust, that I quickly dismiss the idea. With that, I collect my bag from the couch and make my exit. When I want to, I can be dramatic, too.

••

"Did you tell her?"

"Not exactly. I had every intention, but she's made up her mind about us. I thought years of friendship would buy me some trust, but I guess I was wrong."

After I left Sylvia's apartment, I called Tony, who answered his phone before the second ring. He proceeded to blitz me with questions that I couldn't answer fast enough for him, so we agreed to meet for a late lunch at the hotel so I could sort it all out with the help of some Chianti.

"So what did you say to her?"

"Oh, I just yelled at her a little, turned things around a bit." Can't decide whether it's a good time to tell him about her *epiphany*. I already feel like a traitor for sneaking around behind her back. It's probably not a good idea to add to the treachery.

"Are you reconsidering our plans because of Sylvia?" He's wringing his hands as he asks the questions. Sweet.

"No, it feels right. I just don't know how she's going to handle it. If our *coincidental* meeting at your office gave her seizures, I don't know how she's going to react to our relationship," I say with air quotes on the word "coincidental."

"This is crazy! She's an intelligent woman. How can she object when she and I are pretty much done with our project, and you and I have a good thing going? You would think she would be happy for you."

Men never get it. Conflicting forces battle fiercely inside me. On the one hand, I want to protect Sylvia from any hurt I could cause her, but then here is this man, sitting in front of me, believing in me, offering the opportunity for a complete overhaul and redirection for my professional life. It feels good. It's been a long time since someone showed such passionate interest in me. In fact, the last person to do so was me.

"She likes you, Tony." Benedict Arnold called; welcome to the Traitors' Club.

"Yeah, sure, like a toothache." He laughs morosely.

"No, no, she does, but she hates herself for liking you. She's phobic about becoming vulnerable again after her divorce.

"Wasn't that years ago?"

"Wounds may heal eventually, but pain can't tell time, especially if you hide it and pretend it doesn't exist. You've stirred something that has been buried deep inside for ages, and she's being forced to face it in order to recognize these new feelings. Poor thing, she doesn't know which end is up."

Tony leans back in his chair and laughs. "I'm sorry, Jo, I don't mean to make light of this, but I'm sure you understand why this is difficult for me to believe. Every time I'm around that crazy woman, I feel awkward and inadequate. Not to mention flummoxed by the fact that I am so attracted to her. Who's the crazier one, huh?" He *is* cute, in an out-of-focus, pathetic sort of way.

"Yeah, you guys are a mess, I agree, but I think today's catastrophe may work in your favor. Right now, she's taking a hard look inside after her tantrum and trying to untangle some emotional knots."

He scratches his head and gives me a look that I can't read. It's something between fear and exhaustion.

"Tony, relax. She'll come around, I'm pretty sure. But one thing, though, when she does, we need to be ready. At this point, I don't have any idea how she will look upon our new venture, but I'm certain she'll be furious that we took this long to tell her."

"We? Not we. I've been asking you to involve her from the beginning."

"Fine. I did it. I'm just so hurt that she would immediately jump to the wrong conclusion, I can't fight this need to punish her. In any case, we'll have to be clever and firm in our resolve."

His expression tells me he's not buying it. If I push too hard, he might throw in the towel out of some sense of obligation toward her, and I'm not about to let go of this opportunity.

I lean over and put my hand on his knee. "It's going to be great. Don't give up on her. Trust me."

"Oh geez, nothing good ever followed those words. I don't know. She's a lot of work. I don't think I've ever had to work this hard at anything."

"Perhaps nothing's ever been worth the effort."

He looks off into a spot beyond where I sit, his lips split into a warm smile, and he blushes a little.

"Okay, the more we dwell on Sylvia, the more power we give her over our decisions," I say. "I'm ready for a fresh start. What's on the agenda for this weekend? I want to take advantage of every minute before you go back to New York to pitch our idea."

●●●

*I*t's nice to see all of us together. It hasn't happened for a while. In the bustle of performing our individual tasks to get ready for the community center benefit and Grace's wedding, our little group has become a bit deconstructed. Miraculously, Grace agreed to let us be a part of her hair-and-makeup practice session. Considering the magnitude of the opportunity, we vowed to make dinner afterward a priority to catch up on everything, especially the imminent benefit, which is the reason we are *all* indulging in some spa TLC. I, however, have another reason. I'm electrified with both excitement and terror. I'm taking a mammoth leap of faith, but I've decided to fly to New York with Tony. I'm having a very difficult time making decisions about my professional future, and I think this trip could fill in some blanks for me.

The only rope tethering me is the horrific chance that Sylvia might find out about it. None of these new happenings in my life are more important than my friendship with Sylvia.

I intended to disappear without telling anyone until I returned with some solid choices made. But then, the day after Tony invited me, Ursula called to ask for ideas about what to get Grace as a wedding gift, and I blurted it out even before she finished her rhetorical, "Hey, what's going on?"

"I'm going to New York with Tony." The moment the words came out of my mouth, I regretted speaking them.

"Wait, what? Who's Tony? Sylvia's Tony?" The last two words were said with a shudder. "Omigod! Why?" Ursula may not dine with us once a month, but she's like mission control. Every bit of information is eventually transmitted to her to keep her up to speed. She knew there was a man named Tony circling Sylvia.

I told her the whole story of how I became Tony's intercessor with Sylvia, and how, in the process, we found out we had a lot in common, and I said something about our shared vision for the future, although I kept the details about our potential business venture to myself, and how bringing him and Sylvia together suddenly became secondary in importance because she didn't even want him in the first place. I also withheld the tiny detail about Sylvia admitting that she does like Tony. Why? Because it was said in confidence or because I want to appear blameless?

"This is so twisted, Jo. Why is this a problem if she's not interested in him? So he came to work with her, he met you, and you guys like to hang out together, it happens."

"I know, right? It doesn't sound like a problem, but still, she'll flip when she finds out."

"Just don't give up on her. Be the friend you want her to be."

Solid-gold words. I wanted to, really, but was I to lose an opportunity that was dropped in my lap to save Sylvia from her own mixed-up feelings? What if I sacrificed this moment and spent the rest of my life wondering and resenting her?

"I'll do my best, Ursula, I promise."

"So what are you and your *boyfriend* going to do in New York?"

"Are you trying to be funny?"

"Yes, but it sounded creepy when I heard it. Sorry. Okay, tell me this. Sylvia aside, what do you two have going on? Are you friends, are you more than friends, do you want him as a lover, what?"

"Right now, all I can say is that we're friends. There haven't been any serious moves from either of us, just some comfortable flirtation." I'm not ready to tell anyone about my burgeoning professional relationship with him, and I will not be rushed into a premature revelation. It's all in the research stage right now, and what if nothing comes of it?

"I see. But you're going to New York with him." Hearing her tone, gave the whole idea an angle I hadn't wanted to see. "I think you like him more than you're willing to admit. Just like Sylvia."

Those words jolted me into consciousness. What Ursula didn't know was that I already had a clear idea of what is developing between Tony and me. I would not allow myself to be like

Sylvia in any area of my life and hide from the discomforts of change. My parameters for this relationship are hard set. We want to work together on a tv project of our own, and that's it. The big question for me has become, does Sylvia deserve to know all the details, considering her mistrusting behavior of late? Why should I share my plans with her when she has already decided that I betrayed her without giving me an opportunity to let her in on what's really going on? Where did all the years of friendship and loyalty go?

"Ursula, you may think it's a bad idea, but I'm going to New York. If for nothing else than to confirm my view of this situation." *But I hope you don't think too badly of me.*

"I don't think it's a bad idea. If I hadn't taken some killer risks in my life, I wouldn't be where I am now. Go."

On my way to the wall of high-backed, pearl white pedicure chairs, I listen to the bride-to-be explain her vision of what her hair should look like on the big day. I peek into the facials room and smile at the sight of Peggy and Mindy in adjoining beds, with some sort of Dead Sea black mud masks on their faces and cold compresses on their eyes, in lively conversation about all the changes to be made at the community center.

"I don't think your definition of 'beach waves' is the same as mine, Stacey." I hear Grace getting into a serious debate with the stylist about the difference between "beach waves" and the Shirley Temple ringlets now bouncing on one side of her head. She looks at me and cries, "I look like Bette Davis in that creepy Baby Jane movie!"

"Scarier," I say, shaking my head. It's very hard not to burst out laughing, but I manage to give her a look of empathy.

My chair faces the double doors, and when I see Sylvia come in, my stomach muscles tighten. She kisses Grace hello and says a few words to the stylist, which seem to be just the right ones because she promptly sprays water on the creepy curls to dissolve them. I watch Sylvia disappear to the back, I presume to greet Peggy and Mindy. My body relaxes just a bit before she returns, and then she stops, takes off her Bulgari, Jackie-O sunglasses, holds my stare for an interminable two seconds, and, surprisingly, sits in the chair next to mine. The stare turned every drop of my blood to ice.

"Where are we going for dinner?" She says with no hello, no kiss.

"I don't think we've decided. Actually, Maddie's not even here yet." A fact I hadn't noticed until that very instant. "Grace, have you heard from Maddie?" I call across the salon floor. Grace turns slightly and shakes her head. Maddie is notorious for being fashionably late, but today she's officially missing. Before Grace turns back to the mirror, Sylvia is already on the phone with Maddie.

"Ah, now come on, Madeline, we planned this over a week ago. How can you not have someone to watch Iris? Can't you drop her off at your in-laws'?" Only Sylvia would have the guts to manage the Montiels' lives unsolicited.

"I'm not falling for that, Maddie. I think you just don't want to come. If that's it, just say so." Grace shakes off Stacey's hand from her hair and turns completely toward us to hear Sylvia.

"Fine, then just meet us for dinner. By that time, Rich should be available to take her. Good. That's my girl. We'll see you then." She ends the call and places her feet in the tub of swirling water.

"What was that about?" a visibly concerned Grace asks from her chair.

"Oh, I don't know," Sylvia says with a sigh, leaning back on the headrest and closing her eyes. "She was making a bunch of excuses for not coming. I convinced her to at least come for dinner." Grace turns her head slowly back to the mirror, which reflects the quizzical expression on her face. I find it strange too. I've never known Maddie to say no to a day of preening and spoiling herself.

"So how have you been lately?" I ask Sylvia casually, I hope. "When you called to set up this get-together there wasn't much time to talk." The truth is she was very short and to the point when she called about the spa day.

"Busy. We had to redesign an entire issue about ten seconds before the deadline because of a blasted typhoon in Thailand, but I guess it's all in a day's work," she says while she checks the pedicurist's progress. "How's Tony?"

Wow! No warning, no subtle approach to the subject, straight from the hip. "I couldn't say. Did you two finish up the piece?" There, throw it back at her.

"I saw the rough cut, I wrote him an email with the changes I wanted made, and that was the end of that. I assume he's gone back to New York by now, and I assume you said your good-byes."

"You assume a lot of things." I suspect the truce is over.

"Maybe 'assume' is the wrong word. Maybe I should say that I *conclude* these things based on my observations." Her eyes are open, aimed at me, and shooting daggers.

"What you call observation I still call assumption. You can't go through life thinking you know everything because of scenarios you create in your head." I hear the defensive tone in my voice and it's coming out a lot harsher than the situation demands. Is it the guilt I carry for not telling her the whole truth and putting an end to this unnecessary rift between us?

"Oh, so I imagined you at O'Malley's? And I imagined you visiting his office and having dinners with him? That's just what I've seen with my own eyes. Don't make me say what I think went on when I wasn't looking!" She violently pulls one foot out of the pedicurist's hand, risking a laceration, and the other from the water and begins to get up, as if she can't stand to be near me for another minute. My toenails have a fresh coat of nail polish on them, but I just can't let this go. Forty-five-year-old Jo is not much different from sixteen-year-old Jo.

Peggy and Mindy emerge with rosy, refreshed faces from their Zen hideout and into the main floor. What they stumble upon is a pitifully comical scene in which I follow Sylvia as she tries to get away from me, both of us waddling through the establishment on our bare wet heels, flailing our arms for balance like scarecrows come to life.

"Don't you walk away from me, Sylvia. I'm tired of you spitting out what you believe to be the truth and dismissing me. We're going to settle this once and for all!" We disappear into the inner rooms but not before I glance back and notice the horrified looks of the patrons, especially our three friends, Grace from her chair, Peggy and Mindy with their towel turbans, mouths open, eyes widened to the size of golf balls.

By the time I catch up with Sylvia, I'm so embarrassed that I don't even care about the argument. I slump into a sofa in the small waiting area outside the massage rooms, which luckily is empty except for a livid Sylvia pouring iced tea into a glass from a table filled with pitchers of cool drinks and platters of biscotti. When she turns around, her lips part, and I know she's about to begin her rant again. I gesture with my hand for her to stop even before she utters the first word.

"That's enough," I say, defeated. "This is now beyond ridiculous. I'm not even sure why we're fighting. I've tried to understand, but I'm sorry, Sylvia, I don't." I slowly come to my feet and face her evenly. "It's clear that in spite of the fact that you were attracted to Tony, you wouldn't allow yourself to follow your heart. Fine, I respect that. But then, please stop trying to manage what goes on between him and me. You haven't even given me a chance to tell you the whole story."

I circle around her and fill a glass of my own with lemon water. My mouth is dry and I'm shaking. "Yes, he and I have become good friends, just friends. And I don't see the sin or the betrayal or the disrespect in that. I'm going to nurture my relationship with him, I'm going to continue seeing him, but please know that I'm not choosing him over you. Before I tell you about Tony and me, I want you to say that you trust me no matter what. Be my friend and let go of your suspicions. If you can't, I will be very sorry and sad to lose you, but it won't be my doing. My conscience is clear."

Why didn't I just tell her? Why is it so important that she proves herself to me before I can confide in her? Hurt feelings aside, I'm just as bad as she is. Worse, because I have the knowledge, and I'm being deliberately unfair. She only has limited information.

Sylvia puts her glass down gently on the table and without a word leaves the room. I follow her a few seconds later, just in time to see her slide her wet feet into her sandals, hang her purse on her shoulder, and walk out the door.

Nothing brings women together like a day at the spa.

Peggy

•

"Don't stare at them, Peggy!" Mindy whispers from the side of her mouth. She's turned toward a mirror and pretending to rearrange her terry cloth robe, but I just can't take my eyes off the spectacle before me. Sylvia just whizzed by me, clearly trying to get away from a screaming Jo, both clumsily waddling into the private rooms. Not in a million years could I imagine these two making such a public fuss. I feared this dysfunction between Sylvia and Jo would tarnish our fun. I'd been looking forward to this all week. If these ladies only knew how their company helps in healing the ache in my lonely heart.

The next hour is a blur. Grace's eyes are closed while the makeup man is working on her cheeks. Her chest heaves in a huge sigh. About ten minutes after the altercation, Sylvia is gone, and Jo is back in her chair watching intently as her pedicure gets repaired. Mindy discreetly gestures for me to join her in the back to retrieve our clothes. Even the lively female chatter, now reduced to a gentle murmur, is almost drowned out by a multitude of humming handheld hair dryers. By the time my mind clears from the shock, the four of us are sitting at lunch stunned and scratching our heads.

What the heck just happened? An hour ago, we were all enjoying ourselves at the salon. Now, we sit at this table hoping Jo will voluntarily explain her drama with Sylvia and why she skipped lunch. We all hide behind our menus, and I'm startled when Mindy's phone breaks the thick silence.

"Oh hi, Maddie. We're at Seasons 52, down the block from the spa ... No, we haven't ordered yet so you're right on time ... Okay, see you in a bit." She hangs up and says, "I guess we can order our drinks. Maddie's looking for parking. What was that drink you said you love here, Grace?"

Nicely done, Mindy. Someone had to break the ice.

"Um ... the Superfruit Martini."

As if prompted, the waiter arrives just in time to hear Grace. "One Superfruit Martini?"

"Make it five, and leave the shakers on the table, please." We all chuckle tentatively. Maybe we don't have to know what's going on with Sylvia and Jo. Maybe we can just have a nice lunch and let things sort themselves out. After all, it's no one's business but theirs.

Maddie offers a collective hello just as the waiter approaches with our elixir of peace. We place our orders, and the table once again falls into overwhelming silence.

"Here's to the bride and to what I'm sure is going to be a stupendous wedding." Mindy raises her glass and we all follow faithfully. After a long and savored sip of our drinks, I sense that we may still be able to recover our afternoon.

"I like the hair and the makeup, Grace. Is that what you wanted?" I say, emboldened by the warmth of the alcohol in my throat.

"The hair's a little stiff, but it looks good, and I think the makeup will work."

The conversation almost sounds scripted, but I'm holding on to the hope that the vodka will cure us of this awkwardness.

"Is Jack nervous?" My attempt at sounding casual is exaggerated, my tone almost singsong. "The day is coming near." I can't let Mindy do this alone, and Jo and Maddie are strangely quiet.

"If he is, he's not showing it. He's more nervous about the fund-raiser. He keeps going back and forth with Sylvia about whether he wants to be the first or the last to speak."

"Where is Sylvia, by the way?" Maddie asks. "I called her cell before I called Mindy and it went straight to voicemail."

Oh no. I forgot Maddie wasn't there to witness the Battle of the Waddle. We were so close. I can see the enormous effort we're all making not to look to Jo for an answer, but the impulse is too strong.

"She lost her appetite suddenly," Jo says acidly and empties her martini glass. Grace's lips part to say something, but the waiter arrives with our lunch and she stops herself.

"I missed something, I can tell. What's going on?" Maddie won't let it go.

"For some reason, Sylvia doesn't think it's a good idea for me to be friends with Tony Clifton, and I strongly disagree. That's it in a nutshell." Jo begins to pick at the mushrooms on her pork tenderloin medallions.

"When you say friends ..." I murmur almost to myself.

"Friends, Peggy, friends. You can take it to mean whatever you want, and I can mean it in any way I want. Goodness, we're all adults here, aren't we? I can have a scone or a screw with the man and it's nobody's business. Last I checked, no one had any claims on him, so what's the problem?"

"Did you ask Sylvia that?"

"Of course I did! And unless she has a solid reason why I shouldn't see him, I don't intend to stop."

"And are you having a scone or a screw?" My question is delivered gently, but still, I went too far. Jo gives me a look that reminds me of that night when my relationship with my mother took an irreversible turn. There's fury in her eyes, but there's also pain. There's indignation but also disappointment.

"Okay, okay, that's enough. Let's eat." Mindy plays with her sea scallops and makes them dance around in the plate, but she isn't taking a bite.

"Right, I'm sorry Jo. That was out of line. I was trying to make light of this, and it was in bad taste." Her eyes shine like diamonds with repressed tears, but she manages to nod in my direction.

"Let's talk about the shower." Mindy makes a sharp turn like nobody I've ever met. Must be a lawyer thing. "Maddie, Fanny wants us to be at her house about an hour early to help decorate the tables. If you want, I'll pick you up."

Maddie swallows her mouthful of sesame grilled salmon with some difficulty. "Actually, I may not make it. Sorry, Grace. I meant to talk to you about it, but it's been hectic, and I haven't…"

"What do you mean you may not make it? We've been planning this for three months." Grace's face is a mask of panic.

"I know, I know. I didn't expect this to happen, but Rich will be out of town that weekend, so I'll have the kids."

"What about your in-laws? They always watch the kids for you," I interject. It may not sound like it, but I really am trying to help.

"They're busy that weekend, Peggy," she spits at me with mild viciousness.

I'm not buying it, but I'd better shut up before I trip over my tongue again. I refuse to believe that this bomb would drop now, as we begin a season of celebration for an event that has become the manifestation of all our collective dreams.

"Fine. I understand. It's not a big deal." Grace is barely able to formulate the words clearly and they run over each other in a mumble. She looks at Maddie as if reading her, decoding her secret thoughts in search of the true reason for the sudden punishment. Yet I see in their eyes the spark of understanding, looks that say *I can see right through you.*

• •

I don't submit to the societal imperative to procreate, and I don't believe everyone is called to have kids. No regrets in that department. In fact, it would do all women good to self-assess and determine whether raising children is for them. We do a disservice to humanity when we bring children into the world and then decide we weren't cut out for it. I feel fortunate that I know myself enough to spare any child my forced motherhood.

Why, then, did I continue for so long to smile and make polite or witty excuses for never marrying or having kids? The looks of pity, the fumbled words of feigned admiration for my courageous choices. It all became so tiresome. After a while, my responses also became trite and robotic. After a while, you just don't care.

Just like I don't care what people think about my relationship with Mackenzie. So what if I spend too much time with him? So what if I've become too attached? So what? The boy has found purpose and motivation in tennis, but what he has brought to me cannot be put into words. It's respect, it's life, it's meaning.

"That was a gangsta move, Ms. Paulson!" he yells across from the net with eyes as big as eight balls. His thin face breaks into a smile, and he pushes the disheveled soft curls off his forehead with his forearm.

"Thank you! That *was* quite a fake-out," I say with a theatrical bow. "Okay, we'll play the tiebreaker set another day. I have a pile of paperwork waiting for me at home." As soon as I finish the sentence, Mackenzie's semblance changes radically. The excitement, the adrenaline, plummet almost instantaneously. As he makes his way to the benches that face the court, his racket taps the top of the net repeatedly with a hint of harshness in every strike.

I'm disturbed by the amount of time I spend wondering what lurks beneath this boy's exterior, but I'm also terrified to look behind that veil. I must, though, if he is to go where he can go with his talent. Is today the day I place myself firmly in a position to take him to those places, or the day I push him away and undo what little I have accomplished?

"What's with the face, Mac? Sore loser?"

"Nah, I can take you, Ms. P." He attempts a half smile when he joins me on the bench.

"You want a ride?"

"No, I'm gonna hang out here some more."

"It's after seven on a school night. You must have homework."

"It's in my backpack. I can do it here."

"The community center closes at nine. How're you going to get home? What's up, Mackenzie?" There, I did it. I asked.

"Nothing," he answers, turned entirely away from me. And he took too long to say it.

"Come on, Mac. You have to know you can trust me." He faces me finally, his lips part and then close again. "Tell me." I push as gently as I can.

He looks down at his shoes and tugs distractedly at the frayed laces. "I don't wanna. It's not a big deal."

"But there *is* something. Listen, you're a smart kid. You know ignoring whatever it is that's bothering you is not going to make it go away or help you deal with it. Maybe we can find a solution together. But you have to talk about it. Don't hide it. Everything is scarier in the dark." I smile at him and place my hand on his.

"I know what kind of solution you're gonna give me. You're gonna wanna tell someone and you'll end up making it worse."

"You know me better than that. Whatever you tell me will stay only between us if that's what you want. You have my word."

He sighs with exasperation and turns to face me. "Okay, you wanna talk about it, Ms. Paulson? Let's talk about it." There's a brilliance in his eyes that goes beyond the tears he's trying to fight. Old wounds that haven't healed. Knowledge no seventeen-year-old should possess.

"Today is Monday. It's my mom's day off. I'd like to go home and ask her if we could go get some new tennis shoes but she's gonna say no. She might even tell me to go somewhere for a while and let her be. It all depends on her plans for the day. She could be alone at home drinking her paycheck until I have to drag her to her bed in the middle of the night. Or even better, she could be drinking with her douchebag boyfriend. One or the other, I'll just be in the way, and there'll be no money left for shoes. There never is."

The pain that indwells this boy is so deep it has no beginning or end. When the teenager goes, he will leave it behind for the man to carry, and when the man grows older and gives way to the senior, this heartache will sit heavily on his chest every time the memory of his childhood is conjured.

I must tread lightly at this moment. I'm not sure whether he wants a reaction to this confession or just to make the whole conversation die.

"You know, tennis shoes are my addiction. I have too many, but I've been wanting a pair in orange. Let's go get some." Out of the corner of my eye, I see him smile and dry his eyes with his sleeve. Good call.

"No, Ms. P. I know what you're doing, and I can't let you buy me shoes. These just need some new laces and they'll be a'right."

"Who says they're for free? You're going to pay me back. I need help in the laundry facilities at the college, and I've just been dreading the idea of looking for someone to do it. Two evenings a week washing towels and workout gear for two hours, twenty-five dollars a day. What do you think?"

Fist pump.

•••

I recognize the benefits of living in this era of technology, but the unfortunate fallout is that it gives humanity an excuse to remain distant, have sterile, electronic interaction, and still call it a relationship. I am grateful to Skype for the ability to at least look at my grandniece's face on my laptop screen as she regales me with her latest accomplishment on the flute. To many people, that would be enough. It just makes me yearn to hold her even more. When Patricia is finished, and the appropriate *bravos* are offered, my sister and I begin our half-hearted, disengaged dialogue.

"Penny, do you have Mom's string of pearls? I'd like to wear it to a wedding."

"I'd have to look for them. I haven't seen them since I brought Mom's things to the house. They must be in one of the boxes in the attic."

"You should keep them somewhere safe. Those are real, you know? I remember when Dad gave them to her that one Christmas. I thought they were so pretty on her."

"I remember that she wanted diamond studs. Since when do you wear pearls, anyway? They don't exactly go with gym clothes." She laughs a harsh, mocking laugh.

"Is that necessary?"

"Oh, come on, lighten up, I'm kidding. Patricia, take that flute in the bedroom. I can't take it anymore!" She turns abruptly to yell at her unseen granddaughter.

"So, can you send me the pearls? I'll pay for the shipping."

"I'll do my best Margaret, but I've got my hands full watching Patricia and Chester every afternoon so their mother can take her drawing class. Besides, the attic creeps me out. I'll have to wait for Charles to help me find them."

"Harry's wife is taking a drawing class?"

"She's getting her degree in fashion design." Poetic justice. I flash back to Penny's elaborate tales of moving to New York to attend design school and meet rich, cultured people, Mom giggling with delight and believing every word. Now Penny has a front-row seat as her daughter-in-law takes ownership of her once-upon-a-time dreams.

"The wedding is in a month. I think that gives you plenty of time to find the pearls. Penny, this is important to me."

"I said I'd do my best. For heaven's sake, Margaret, it's just a necklace."

Here we go again. We're blood, we're twins. How can she have such complete disregard for everything that is meaningful to me? I feel the temperature rising in my veins.

"Quit dismissing me, Penny. I don't ever ask you for anything, I stay away from your family every time you give me one of your sorry excuses so I won't go visit your kids and grandkids even though they're my family too. You don't care an ounce about me. I don't get it, but I've learned to live with it." My voice is at a fevered pitch now, and I can hardly recognize myself, but I can't stop. Penny's eyes are as wide as an owl's and she doesn't seem to hear the flute resuming in the background.

"I'm only asking for one thing that is no skin off your back. You don't even care about the blessed pearls. You need to find a hobby other than using my feelings for target practice." Boy, that felt good.

I don't think I took a breath during that entire blast. I refill my lungs and notice that now Penny's eyes are as narrow as incisions. She looks behind her to check on Patricia's location and gets so close to her computer, her face swells on my screen. I know that look. She's about to attack.

"You're right about one thing: I will never understand how you and I can be related, let alone twins," she whispers viciously. "You were nothing but a disappointment to Mom, and Dad felt sorry for you. Have you come out of the closet yet? You don't have to hide anymore, right? They're both dead now." Her mouth foams with judgment and contempt.

I take in her words and register my emotions. I don't want to, but I can't help myself.

"And if it wasn't for Charles," I answer, "you'd still be a mediocre receptionist trawling for men from Friday to

Monday. So which one of their princesses do you think would make Mom and Dad prouder, the lesbian or the whore?" I had to retaliate.

And then, a revelation.

"Patricia! Shut up with that damn flute! NOW!" she shouts, picks up a glass of wine that up to now was outside the range of my screen, and knocks back the entire thing. She's drunk. Not buzzed or mellow. Bitter, fed-up, malcontented drunk.

If our conversations were disheartening before, we may never recover from this one. I am so alone. Nobody knows me, least of all my sister. I don't know myself either, I fear. Who is this woman screaming indignities at a laptop?

My heart aches, and I hear its forlorn beating in my temples. Hot tears begin to burn the corners of my eyes. I will let them flow. So many reasons to grieve. Audible sobs escape my lips and I surrender. I grieve for me, I grieve for my parents, for Mackenzie. I grieve the most for my sister.

Mindy

•

I think I like Margolis's office. It's everything I would want mine to be, if I wanted to be a shady, double-dealing attorney. I shouldn't say that. Margolies is one of the most sought-after divorce attorneys in this town and other prominent cities in the country. He is our biggest competitor for high-profile cases. That said, he's still shady.

The dark-paneled walls in this conference room give an unsettling vibe, intentionally, no doubt. Everything is dim and austere. This tall black leather chair is comfortable but seems to swallow me no matter how much I try sitting up straight. Elegant water goblets are set around the table, and in the middle of the mahogany vastness is a pitcher of ice-cold water. No windows. Nothing but artificial light from recessed fixtures in the ceiling that illuminate the tabletop but keep the rest of the room in shadows. That I don't like. Even my closet of an office has a small window. An antiseptic smell fills my nostrils. It triggers the same sensation I get when I go to the dentist.

Come on, let's get this over with. I know what they're doing, and I'm a little offended. Don't they know I recognize the old psychological trick of making someone wait? I hear a constant low murmur of voices right outside the door, but no one enters.

I've already checked emails on my phone three times, but I keep looking up at the massive clock on the wall, and it's making the time go even slower. *Patience, Johnson.* Let's see how superior they feel after I work my magic.

I hear the swish of the door against the carpet, and in parade Margolies and his partner, flanking Montiel. My instinct is to get up, but I stifle it. Let them come to me. I'm still a lady, although they won't call me that when I'm done with them.

"Who is this Mason Davis?" There's a fireworks display going on in Montiel's angry eyes.

"Forensic accountant, Mr. Montiel. My firm hired his team to make sure that we had all pertinent details, so we could reach a speedy settlement with little contention. Also, we thought they could advise us on the long-term financial and tax impact of whatever divorce settlement option we choose."

"I thought all this had already been decided, Margolies. Why are we chewing on this again?"

I feel sorry for the opposing counsel right now. He looks despondent. With every case I feel less and less satisfaction staging these attacks. I'll break the awkward silence.

"It's all my fault. When your paperwork finally arrived in my office, it seemed disorganized and incomplete to me. I thought trying to figure it all out on my own would be more time-consuming." *Poor little ol' me.*

"I'm not paying for it. I agreed to pay all the legal costs, but I wasn't told about these accountants, so I'm not paying for it."

"Fair enough, Mr. Montiel. They're on me. Now, if we could proceed, I would like to explain the report from the Davis team. Some of their findings include certain assets held in trusts of various types and terms, several small accounts in different countries, and one very significant asset in Germany in the form of a residential and commercial real estate company by the name of … yes, here it is: Zuhause/Geschäft, GmbH. Not to mention the very pricey properties your German corporation purchased in several locations in Europe. My confusion upon initially reviewing your financial disclosures stemmed from a distinct impression I had that something had been, how shall I say it, manipulated, for lack of a better word. Considering I have known you personally for some time now, I assured Mr. Davis and his team that nothing underhanded should be suspected, and that perhaps these omitted details were just an oversight, seeing as you established these international corporations quite some time ago."

Montiel's normally beady eyes are marbles now, and Margolies drops his head, perhaps in prayer. "Well, Mindy, Ms. Johnson, I also will need my attorneys to review this laundry list you've handed me before I agree to any settlement. I guess this will take longer than we thought."

"Actually, the good news is that anything these accountants present, based on their investigation, will probably carry a lot of weight in court, so I don't believe your attorneys will have too many objections. You see, hiring Mr. Davis and his team saved us all some time." I punctuate this last piece of information with an enthusiastic smile that says, *I've done us all a favor.*

Margolies does a prudent amount of paper-shuffling to keep up appearances and attempts to push back once again. "Ms. Johnson, this forensic report is thorough and taking the information contained in it into consideration, I'm sure that we can come to an agreement that is satisfactory to both Mr. and Mrs. Montiel. However, I would ask that we review this settlement you propose. It seems quite excessive."

I'm unmoved. "Mr. Margolies, I realize you haven't had sufficient time to review the report properly, but I assure you that every asset presented by Mr. Montiel, and those unearthed later, were expertly valuated by the Davis team. My proposal, you will find, is quite fair in view of the circumstances."

If I had to describe Margolis's facial expression and the exchange of glances between him and his mute partner in one word, I would have to go with *concession.* Checkmate.

••

I don't like meeting clients in my office. The ultramodern conference room at the firm helps perpetuate my efficacious attorney persona much better than my workspace. It's small and disturbingly cluttered. I could say that I don't have a lot of room because frankly, my office is more like a sealed cubicle, but it's not a solid defense for the chaos. I've never understood the practice of having endless tomes of law books in attorneys' offices. Apparently, that gives you almost as much credibility as your diploma on the wall, so I have them. Never read them. I do all my research online. They're just decoration, and in this office, not even that. They lie strewn and dusty in no particular order, different sets mixed in together with no regard for sequence. Piles of paper rise sporadically from almost every flat surface. To a stranger's eyes, it might look like a severe delay in the management and filing of important paperwork, given the setting, but on closer inspection, the papers are nothing but old periodicals and junk mail. I keep the important paperwork in stacks of folders that clutter the area between my chair and the window behind it.

In stark contrast to the rest of my office, my desk is impeccable every morning. Nilda, my magical elf, always makes sure I start my day with a perfectly organized desk.

She thinks I don't notice how she positions my favorite pens precisely perpendicular to the left edge of the pristine surface. And every morning I choose to look at nothing but that.

When Maddie arrives, she has to navigate several piles, over hill and over dale, in the obstacle course between the door and my desk, and I have to choke laughter. There is a twinge of guilt, not because of the mess but because I find mirth in the situation rather than feel embarrassment.

"I'm not going to lie, Mindy. I'm a little nervous."

"I don't know why. I told you I'd take care of you."

"Yes, and I trust you, but you were so cryptic when you asked me to come. Up until now, you never had a problem giving me updates on the phone."

"Well, some things are better explained face to face. It's all done, Maddie. I have an offer here from Richard's attorney that I don't think requires any further negotiation."

I hand her a draft of the settlement with all the delightful details of my triumph. Nevertheless, she seems baffled, and her eyes don't seem to be focusing. I walk around my desk and sit next to her.

"I'm sorry, what does this all mean? What is Zuhause/Geschäft, GmbH?"

"That, my friend, is your ticket, your gold mine. That's what's going to set you up for the rest of your life."

I proceed to tell her all about my meeting with Montiel and his attorney, and I don't think she blinks once while I'm talking. She is lost in a haze of bewilderment, laboring to understand.

"So … can I keep my house?"

I feel a twinge of tenderness for her. She can't comprehend the scope of this victory.

"Sweetie, yes, you can keep the house, and just to give you an idea of what else you're going to get, you'll be able to pay for two PhDs and a small island, if that's what you want."

Her smile tells me the fog is beginning to lift even if her eyes are bursting with tears.

"Well, if that's all you could manage, it will have to do." We both laugh, and she throws her arms around me in a tight and long embrace. "Let's celebrate."

"Oh no, I can't. This is the first day this week I don't have to go to court, and I have a mountain of paperwork to do, including polishing up your final documents. By the way, you may want to start thinking about what you want to do about taxes on future income."

"I'm getting overwhelmed again. Come on, Mindy, it's after one o'clock. Suddenly I'm starving, and you know, friends don't let friends drink alone. I'll think about all that later. Tomorrow is another day."

I don't have the heart to refuse her when she's asking me to join her on what is probably her first worry-free meal in a long time. So, with a deep exhale, I give in.

"Fine, Scarlett O'Hara, but you're buying."

•••

"Mister Soto want to see you in his office, Mindy." Nilda whispers his name in exaggerated reverence.

My reliance on procrastination has never served me well, but I just never learn. Once I made the final and risky decision on my professional future, my intention was to precede my resignation email with a face-to-face conversation. I'm sensing it was not a good idea to put that off so long that I ended up having to send an official communication to give sufficient notice. I'm just not good at human resources protocol.

I have a strong suspicion that Gerardo Soto buys his suits in the children's department. He's barely over five feet and wears his thick black hair slicked back, and when I say slicked, I mean oil-spill slick. He always wears pin-striped suits. Even at the annual charity golf tournament sponsored by the firm, he wears thin-striped shorts. Maybe he thinks the vertical lines make him look taller.

The word most often used by clients and office staff to describe him is *charming*. He is disciplined about controlling his inevitable Napoleon complex. It surfaces in all its blistering glory only when things don't go his way, which is not often.

"Mr. Soto, you wanted to see me?"

"Didn't really want to, but have to, Miss Johnson."

Uh oh. I haven't been "Miss Johnson" since he hired me.

"I understand you have decided to leave the firm."

"Yes, sir. I've been doing a lot of soul-searching for a while now, and I feel I have contributed as much as I can to the firm. I've reached a stage in my professional life where I hear other pursuits calling. I assure you that it's been a struggle to make this decision. I've been very happy here, but at this juncture, if I stay just for comfort and don't take a chance, eventually the 'what-ifs' would compromise the quality of my work. I feel if I can't give 100 percent to the job, it's not fair to stay any longer." To my ear, it all sounds like a pathetic stumble through the points I want to make to justify my leaving.

"Hogwash. Nothing but excuses, Mindy. I'll tell you what I think. I think you're delusional and tangled up in hypocritical scruples. You're leaving one of the most successful law practices on the East Coast to go manage a decaying community center. You'll be a laughing stock in legal circles."

His words send chills up my spine. I don't give a tiny rat's ass what people think of me in legal circles, but to hear him speak my choice with such contempt, is unsettling. I'd be fooling myself if I didn't have to catch my breath every time I thought about not taking the DC job to put all my professional and emotional stock into the community center.

"How do you know ...?"

"Oh, come on, did you really think it wouldn't get back to me?"

I am stunned. Not because he knows but at my own stupidity for believing he wouldn't find out. "Mr. Soto, I can't possibly convey to you how sorry I am, but I don't think it's necessary for you to be insulting. As I explained in the email, I'm convinced that it's time for me to explore other professional paths. I trust that you can respect my decision."

"I'm disappointed, more in myself than in you. You came highly recommended, and you have done a tremendous job here. I had many plans for you."

"Sir, I'm very sorry that I've become a disappointment to you. It was never my intention to embarrass you. I simply feel the urge to make a radical professional move."

"Your desire to explore other professional areas is not the reason for my indignation, Miss Johnson. I sold you to the senior partners as if you were the holy grail of law. I put in your name for junior partner."

The weight of his words crushes me. "Why?" I can barely ask the question. "I never asked to be considered for partner. Isn't that a requirement? And I haven't been here long enough."

"It doesn't matter now, does it?" He combs his hair with the fingers of both hands with frenetic speed. "Let me tell you something, Miss Johnson, there are two types of birds in this world: the canary and the hawk. If you put both in the same environment, the hawk will eat the canary alive every single time. It's not a kind reality, it's probably not fair, but given a choice, it's always smart to be a hawk. Miss Johnson, you're a canary. Your poise and drive are nothing but affectations."

Not many people outside of my family have ever made me question my identity and my principles. I've always been my own judge. Today, after Gerardo Soto's last words to me, I leave this office a stranger to myself.

"Permission to approach the bench?" That always makes me smile. It's my sister's cute but tentative way of asking if I'm in a listening mood. She interprets the smile as an invitation to come into my room.

"I called you at work. Nilda said you had a rough afternoon and left early."

"There should be a law that days that start well should not end the way this one did. Oh well. I was hoping not to leave on bad terms, but it is what it is."

Momentous decisions that thrust your life forward never come without a price, and perhaps disappointing Messrs. Wasserman, Katz & Soto is the premium I had to pay to find my way. To think less than a week ago I reluctantly agreed to a lunch that would change my professional trajectory. When Maddy and I spoke our triumphant toasts to her freedom, it opened a floodgate of ideas for fresh, meaningful purpose, not just for her but even for me. Gradually, our vision for the community center and our convergence with it became clearer. And just like that, her nursing and my legal backgrounds had new focus.

"Are you sure you want to do this?"

"I'm as sure as I can be. Up until my conversation with Soto, I had butterflies about making such a huge change, but when he said I would be 'a laughing stock in legal circles,' I could've sworn he said 'circus'. That's the moment that sealed it for me. That's what these divorce cases usually are, a circus. My subconscious made up my mind for me. And I'm not even sorry anymore about taking Nilda with me."

"And Washington?"

"That was worse. At least Soto talks straight. He's contentious and dismissive. I understand that language. Talking to the senator was like talking to the Riddler. I never quite figured out what he wanted me to do in that office. People who speak in puzzles unnerve me, and that's all politicians ever do. Besides, I must confess I've been having these daydreams since I came back from DC where Hattie is older and asking me, 'What did I lose to, Tía Mimi? What was so important that you had to sacrifice me?'"

Ruby's tender smile is bathed in pity. She's not buying it.

"I know, hiding behind a four-year-old is the cowardly way of rationalizing my decision."

"So Maddy did well in her divorce?"

"All I'm allowed to tell you is that it's the biggest payoff I've ever gotten for anyone."

"Wow. And she wants to take on the community center? I'd be booking trips all over the world."

"I'm sure she'll do some of that, but the community center is actually a smart idea. Taxes are going to be an issue for Maddie, so being the primary source of income for the center is going to help her a lot. She wants to expand the place with a clinic and a law office. I want to be involved in that. It's exactly what I need and where I need to be. This may be the birth of new careers for both of us."

"I'm glad you're not leaving Miami."

"Are you?"

She looks hurt. "Yes, I am. Mindy, Hattie adores you, and let's face it, I don't think I can raise her without you."

That makes me smile. "I *know* you can't. I wasn't sure you knew it."

Madeline

GALA FOR

OCEAN VIEW COMMUNITY CENTER

Providing support and services to improve community life

PROGRAM

Welcome prayer by

Pastor Maria Cabrera

After the opening prayer, I take one last walk around the ballroom before I sit down, and I overhear comments that make me proud of what we've done. Waiters carrying trays ribbon around the room in an endless conveyor belt of cocktails, weaving through the sea of beautiful dresses and silk-tied suits.

"The centerpieces are stunning."

"I'm bidding on that cruise in the silent auction."

"The music is amazing."

"Who catered this? The food is incredible."

That last one is my favorite. Must tell Jo.

My anxiety level is sky high. I can only stay seated for a few minutes, before I start walking again. I manage to avoid

Rich's table. I see Mercy's arm entwined with his. I walk over to Sylvia and Tony, who are involved in yet another bicker-fest. Her Dresden blue and silver gown is an art deco masterpiece.

"Don't forget to talk to Grace and Jack. They're slippery and don't like a lot of attention. And Grace hates pictures." She talks to the photographer shadowing Tony. "She'll want to check every picture you take of her. Just humor her. She comes with a manual, that one."

"Anything else, Herr Kommandant?" Tony clicks his heels to attention.

"Very funny. I need a drink." She's nervous and excited, as always.

"Get me one, will you?"

"Should you be drinking?" She pivots to glare at him.

"May I remind you, I'm not on the clock, and I know I have a task to accomplish."

"Fine." She rolls her eyes.

"Champagne, please, not arsenic," he says with a grin as she walks in the direction of the massive bar. "Now that's what I call romance."

I wonder what's going on with these two and Jo. Whatever stage their drama is in, they seem to have put it aside for this event. Or most of it.

For an instant, I'm distracted from my anxiety by the amusement they provide. Certain women take center stage anywhere just by their mere presence. I envy that. Tonight, it's another episode of *The Sylvia Sabatino Show,* but I'm not staying behind the scenes. This forgettable extra is going to make some noise. Although I think I hear a faint voice, far, far away in my head, screaming *worst timing ever.*

As I continue to take in the wonder of this night, I'm reminded of the decision I made last night. I can safely say it was not made in haste. I pondered long and hard as I consulted with Blaze. *Tell me what to do. Give me some direction.* I understood my beagle's gentle snort to mean *you're on your own.*

Dinner Menu

APPETIZER
SEARED BAY SCALLOPS
served over sautéed spinach with sauce Choron

SOUP
TWO-MUSHROOM VELOUTÉ

ENTRÉE
GRILLED CHILEAN SEA BASS
on vegetable ragout and tricolored orzo

WHITE WINE—WEISSBURGUNDER (PINOT BLANC)
Mosel Valley, Germany

or

MEDALLIONS OF BEEF IN RED WINE SAUCE
on vegetable julienne & potato galette with sweet onions

RED WINE—CABERNET-MERLOT
Pfalz, Germany

DESSERT

AMARETTO ICE CREAM TORTE TOPPED WITH SWIRLING
MERINGUE AND FRESH BERRIES

SELECTION
OF INTERNATIONAL
TEAS & COFFEES

AFTER DINNER

FRESH FRUIT & CHEESE SERVED WITH MINI-SWEETS
& CHOCOLATE TRUFFLES

Music courtesy of the Miami Jazz Group

Thanks to the lavish dinner, the general mood is mellow and contented. The musicians play in soft tones with lots of flute and piano, aiding in the digestion of the meal. I, however, have barely picked at my plate. My wineglass has been refilled more times than I can count. I'm just over the "buzzed" level, but my resolve is unshaken, and I must do this fast before one of the other women attempts to neutralize the situation and I lose my nerve. Oh boy, I feel a retail therapy session coming. Tomorrow is going to be a Louis Vuitton day.

I see Grace rise and walk to another table. My gut tells me this is my chance. When I walk over to her, she introduces me to Kimberly Bosworth, I think I heard her say, dean of the English department at the college. I try my very best to offer the proper pretentions of politeness.

We find a secluded corner on the wide wraparound balcony. She sits in one of the thick wicker armchairs, the watercolor flowers in her flowy gown cascading all around it, takes off her slingbacks, and rubs her feet. Lively voices and laughter from the ballroom mix with the serenade of tropical breezes coming from the dancing palm trees surrounding the building.

"Geez, it's muggy out here. Are you okay, Maddie? I noticed you've been staying clear of Rich's table."

"I'm fine. Grace, I don't know if we'll have a chance to talk before the wedding, so it's gotta be now."

She grabs her knees and braces herself. She knows something's coming. "What's up?"

"Why didn't you tell me you went to dinner with Rich and his whore?" The alcohol takes me straight to the point.

She swallows hard and lowers her eyes. "Oh man, what fresh nightmare is this," she mutters mostly to herself.

"It has to be now. I couldn't take another day of looking you in the face without saying something."

"How long have you known?"

The wheels are turning in her mind. I'm not going to let her embroider some lame excuse. She'd better not turn this around on me.

"A few weeks."

"Why didn't you say something before? This is why you were so weird at lunch on spa day."

"Are you seriously blaming me for not bringing it up? You have some nerve."

"Of course not. I should've said something. It wasn't that big a deal. I made it into something by not telling you and I'm sorry, but this isn't the time, Maddie."

"This is the only time. I had to gather courage from where I didn't have it to finish planning your bridal lunch because I had made a commitment, but that's the end of my patience. I'm gonna say what I've been wanting to say now."

"You're drunk. Listen, I get it, you have every right to be upset, but now is not a good time. Look around you, Madeline. We've been working on this for months and there's a lot at stake. I'm going in."

She's getting up. Oh no. She doesn't get to call the shots this time. In a desperate impulse, I lunge for her shoes and dangle them over the balcony.

"Without your shoes? If you're thinking of coming for them, just know that the minute you touch me, I'll let them go. Ihavesomethingstosay…" I hear my words smearing against each other, so I take a breath. "And I don't care what I have to do to make you listen."

She looks around for an escape route, I suppose, so I'd better speak my piece before she bolts, or I lose my nerve. Muffled applause seeps from inside the ballroom. The speeches are starting.

GUEST SPEAKERS

Jack Masters

Associate Professor, Department of Fine Arts (Music)
South Florida College

"Our hope and goal are that rooted in the revival of the community center, the community itself will be strengthened. Let us allow ourselves to dream big. Maybe we can inspire other communities in South Florida to recognize and protect the value of centers like Ocean View ..."

"Do you know how I found out about your new relationship with Rich and his whore? Straight from the whore's mouth. And do you have any idea what that felt like?"

"Madeline, there is no relationship, it was nothing but business. It was an uncomfortable, sycophantic move to stroke your ex-husband's enormous ego so all of this could happen." She points with both arms extended at the ballroom on the other side of the glass.

"That's bull! The whore ... said you ... were love ... ly." It's so hard to be forceful when you hiccup. "That doesn't sound like it was too uncomfortable." I'm losing steam, and my eyes are watering. "But why didn't you ... tell me?" More hiccups, and I hear myself slurring again.

"I don't know, okay? I don't know! I was afraid you'd think I was selling out. Believe me, *I* thought so. I tried a thousand ways to talk Jack out of it, but he just didn't get it. He didn't see how a dinner to discuss the fund-raiser was a betrayal to you."

"Why didn't Jack go by himself?"

"Why didn't Jack and Rich meet alone? Why did Rich insist on taking her and forcing me to go? Why do you think, Maddie?

To create this scene right here, between you and me. He knew it would be inappropriate for Jack to go without me. It was elegant blackmail. You want me to pull strings at the alumni association to help with the fund-raiser, your girlfriend will have to accept mine."

She's angry but not at me, at herself for becoming Rich's pawn. Not many people are successful at manipulating Grace.

"And he won. Look at us, Maddie. You were the first person I told when Jack and I got engaged, and now I guess you've been outside looking in almost the whole time. He won." Her voice quavers.

A chill runs through my spine at her last words. "And after? Why didn't you tell me after? Did you think of me at all?"

"Oh my God, Madeline, STOP! Not everything is about you. I had a few things on my mind, you know? And quite frankly I was dreading this moment. I knew no matter what the reasons, you would not take it well. I'm so tired of tiptoeing around your feelings all the time. I just didn't have the energy for it. And the more time passed, the harder it became to bring it up."

"Do you really think I'm that stupid? Do you really think that a dinner about the fund-raiser would upset me? What made me crazy was having to hear it from her. You should've told me, Grace. That's the kicker. And on top of that, you think I'm so unstable and immature that you couldn't be honest with me." I'm suddenly more clearheaded than I want to be, and my words are sharp.

The door opens and Sylvia, Tony, and Ursula come outside, drinks in hand. Sounds from inside escape into the balcony. For a moment, my attention flutters away toward a familiar voice.

Richard Montiel

CEO of Montiel International
Corporate Sponsor
Member of South Florida College
Alumni Association

"The Ocean View Community Center is a private, nonprofit agency that provides the residents of southwest Miami and surrounding areas with the support, services, and programs to improve community life …"

The tension thickens the already stifling humid air on the balcony. In other parts of the country, September is a month of welcome relief from the heat, but not in Miami. The atmosphere is loaded with moisture, and without a forgiving breeze, any more than a few minutes outdoors can be intolerable.

"Pump your brakes right there, Maddie!" Grace says, raising her hands. "Look at how long you've been keeping this inside.

We've seen each other many times since that dreadful dinner. We talked endlessly about the colors for the wedding cake, and how big, and what shape, and not once did it occur to you to bring this up?"

"Don't turn this around so I'm the one at fault and believe me there were many times when I didn't want to talk about your stupid cake, and I bit my tongue until it bled." *Actually, to be honest, right now I wish we could just end all of this and sit down to talk about your cake, but I think that would compromise the authenticity of my rage.* "You had to be the one to tell me, Grace. Will you at least admit that?" I struggle to stay indignant. There was an earth-shaking shift when she said *he won.* In that instant, I felt it was urgent that we became allies again.

"Girls calm down. People are looking at you." Instinctively, petite Ursula, moves between us and the enormous window in a hopeless attempt to block the scene from the guests inside. "Stop it. We've worked too hard on this to let it all fall apart because of some stupid drama that Rich, the butt boil, has created, no offense, Maddie." She hands Grace her own drink, then takes Tony's glass of champagne and tentatively offers it to me as if it were a loaded gun. I take a sip of the drink, but more alcohol can't possibly be a good idea. Grace shoots a smile at the people inside sitting closest to the window. I see Peggy standing at the podium. My head is fuzzy. I can't let them distract me.

Margaret Paulson

Women's Tennis Assistant Coach
Intercollegiate Athletics Department
South Florida College

"It is a great honor to be here on this wonderful evening for the community center as well as for South Florida College. Our school accepts the responsibility to participate with communities to pursue effective, self-sustaining solutions to its human, social, and economic issues …"

I swig half the champagne in the glass. I feel the shoes hanging precariously from my fingers, and I place them on the ledge. "I can't trust anybody." I hear myself talking to the glass more than to the people standing in front of me. "I've had to go through this nasty divorce in silence. I couldn't talk to anyone. I thought I'd lose my mind."

"You. Are. Not. Serious, Madeline. I've spent the better part of this year up until I got engaged holding your hand. I've been there for you all hours of the day and night. How can you say you had no one to talk to?" Grace's voice is sopping with resentment.

"And then what, Grace? How could you do it? How could you sit in front of that skank knowing everything I went through because of her and hide it from me? *You* don't getta be mad at *me!*" My words are nothing but slurred screeching. I don't want to hear myself anymore.

"I'm going in to get more drinks." Tony exits in extreme discomfort, but out of the corner of my eye, I see him peeking through the window. He wants to watch without getting touched by the ugliness. Men can be such wimps when it comes to confrontation. Ursula puts an arm around me, but I shake it off violently. Sylvia glistens with perspiration. She glistens beautifully. The neckline of her gown is wet, but even under the shine, her makeup is flawless. She's shushing me, which is never a good thing to do to a frantic woman.

"Would it have made a difference, Maddie?" Grace asks. "If I had warned you that I was backed into a wall and had to go with Jack, would you have understood? No, you would've reacted just like this. Telling you would've been the right thing to do, but I'm so tired of being afraid of your emotional reactions. Lately, you're a live grenade all the time."

My eyes burn with angry fire. I hadn't noticed until now that our friends have taken three steps behind Grace, indeed as if waiting for me to detonate. I sense a speck of pleading in Grace's voice, but it's not enough. She should be begging me to forgive her. That's what I want. I deserve that.

In a reflexive move, I don't just push the shoes over the ledge, I throw them forcefully into the abyss, and then hurl my drink squarely in her face. There's an instant of regret, but it vanishes quickly.

Everything has been said. I look at our friends. Sylvia turns her head away as if witnessing a wreck. I see champagne dripping down Grace's face and onto her lips, from her chin and hair onto her dress. What a waste. It's good champagne.

Mackenzie Holloway

Graduating Senior
Coral Sea Senior High School

"To the six ladies who fought together to save the center, I want you to know that my dreams are alive because of your commitment. You are an example of how friendship and unity can accomplish goals, and your bond and loyalty to each other and this center is an inspiration to all of us …"

"I have to go look for my shoes." Grace speaks softly and with dignity. She walks into the ballroom, hair drenched, dress stained. I follow at a distance. I can't help it. I have to see this. Jack interrupts his conversation with Mark and Daisy to watch in horror as his barefoot and bedraggled bride-to-be edges around the tables toward the elevators. People turn away from Mackenzie to stare at her. She speaks.

"What? It's really humid out there!"

ANNOUNCEMENT OF
SILENT AUCTION WINNERS

Sylvia Sabatino
Editor-in-Chief
Vivace! Miami

CLOSING PRAYER

Pastor Maria Cabrera

Josephine

I'm tired. I've been on my feet for almost nine hours straight. I should've had someone help me. The decision to take on the dessert bar for Grace's shower all on my own was not a good one. I haven't worked without an assistant in fifteen years. Right now, I wish I had a job I could do lying down. I do a mental chuckle at the questionable meaning of that thought.

It's almost two in the morning and all is quiet in the ghostly restaurant kitchen, but it's how I like it when I'm experimenting with a new confection or doing paperwork. I look up from my workspace and see a blanket of sweets spread among the three stainless steel tables ahead. Two hundred miniature desserts in twenty different varieties that will spend the night in an enormous fridge, then be packaged at dawn and delivered to Fanny's house. Brown-buttered butterscotch bars, salted *dulce de leche* brownies, rose cakes, little coconut soufflés, individual red velvet cakes monogrammed with gold *G*s and *J*s. I'm doubly exhausted just looking at them, but I smile with pride.

Flashes of my days in culinary school play in front of me, and my laughter echoes in the empty kitchen. Bathing turkey shanks in a butterscotch sauce intended for a pecan bourbon bread pudding; setting a sauté station on fire while reducing a vanilla rum custard; flooding the kitchen because I left the tap running with a stopped sink; stepping on a full stock pot I had left cooling on the floor; the teaching staff rolling their eyes and slapping their foreheads in disbelief. If those chefs could see me now.

I wish Tony could see this. He would be impressed. He's always showering me with adulation, but this sight would make his jaw drop. This is what I call a résumé! And he was astonished at the fund-raiser. I spent more time supervising and directing than socializing, so I appreciated his effort to find me and lavish me with compliments.

Why am I so hell-bent on showing off for him? He's pretty starstruck already, but it feels so good to trigger expressions of worship in him. I can probably draw conclusions about why he's so flattering. It's all about business, I'm not delusional, but I'm enjoying every minute of this wild ride.

I couldn't begin to imagine how to make a fourteen-thousand-square-foot monster mansion into a cozy home, but somehow Fanny has done it. I'd heard that she comes from old money, but taking in my surroundings, I'm still amazed at the scope of her family's wealth. There isn't that much money to be made in event planning, and her pilot husband couldn't possibly make enough for them to sustain this palatial estate on their salaries alone. It's a hidden sanctuary in Miami Beach with sweeping views of the Atlantic, palm trees, scenic walkways, side entrances, fountains, twin staircases in ivory granite and cast-iron railings, coffer ceilings. Her kitchen has nothing to envy my own at the hotel in size and is what a chef's kitchen should be.

When I arrive two hours before the bridal shower guests are expected, I see my work arranged on her counters and empty platters waiting to be adorned with the desserts.

"I was thinking we could use the sunroom for the dessert bar. The sunset will look stunning coming through the windows, and I figure that's about the time we'll be ready for dessert," she says as she walks me to the room where a massive table has been covered in exquisite ivory linen embroidered with delicate gold bows. Subtle music floats throughout the entire house.

Arched windows from floor to ceiling take the place of walls. Every room in this house makes you catch your breath, and yet you would be hard-pressed to guess that a bridal shower is about to take place. At Grace's insistence, none of the predictable decorations are present. No streamers, no banners, no balloons. The food, the table arrangements, the flowers, and the house are sufficient embellishments, for sure. This may be a very casual, low-key shower, not to say uppity or even boring, but I can see how it befits the bride-to-be. I can't picture Grace playing raunchy games or getting a lap dance from a sweaty stripper, and quite frankly, we're all a little old for that.

"I just want a ladies' lunch, nice and simple," she said to the chagrin of some of her rowdier friends. I'm starting to agree with Maddie that Grace's definition of *simple* is not the same as everyone else's. This venue is not simple. Elegant, yes, but not simple.

Promptly at one o'clock, the guests begin to arrive. At first, most of the faces are unfamiliar to me, but soon I see Peggy and Mindy make their way into the grand foyer and between the flanking staircases. Before we're done with our hello kisses and a few shared *oohs* and *aahs* about the house and comments about how beautiful our hostess looks in her last trimester, we hear soft applause and turn to see Grace make her entrance with Fanny, a brilliant smile on her face.

"Congratulations lady, you're almost there." We hug when she finally reaches the three of us.

"I know! This is so surreal. Every time I catch my reflection in a mirror, I tell it *you're getting married, you're getting married.*" Her elation is almost manic, but it's cute in a disturbing sort of way.

Sylvia comes in just as Fanny sweeps Grace away and takes her from cluster to cluster of women to say her hellos and to allow everyone a chance to congratulate her. Sylvia kisses

Grace and hugs her warmly. She kisses all of us, but there is an awkward silence between the two of us, and she quickly excuses herself to get a lychee martini, the signature drink of the festivities.

If you didn't know how good Fanny is at what she does, you might worry about how the dynamic of the shower would work, since colleagues and friends don't really mix in Grace's life. But clearly everything has been orchestrated in a way that everyone seems to have interesting or entertaining things to say, and somehow the joy of celebrating the bride among us is a buffer and the common denominator.

Bottles of wine flow uninterrupted. Several servers weave in and out of the conversation groups offering hors d'oeuvres. I notice that a lot of conversation centers on how the fundraiser was a rousing success. Madeline makes her entrance just a few moments before Fanny announces that the lunch buffet is ready. I imagine we're all feeling the same thing, a sense of relief mixed with cautious joy. I didn't see what happened on that hotel balcony, but after I heard the story from Ursula, I'm glad I missed it, and I wondered whether Maddie would show. She came after all, so perhaps our sense of trouble between her and Grace is unfounded. She greets Fanny first, walks by every group of women, stopping briefly to talk to the people she knows, and politely greets those she doesn't. She then comes to greet Peggy, Mindy, and me and remains for a bit.

"You came." Ursula appears, wide-eyed and making no effort to mask her surprise.

"I was invited."

"I wasn't sure you'd come. You know, after the banquet …"

Maddie cuts her eyes to Ursula and stops the flow of words. Message received. We are not to speak of that night. Fat chance.

"So, are you coming to the wedding?" *Abort, abort, Ursula.*

"Maybe." Maddie's resentment spreads over all of us like an itchy blanket. I get the feeling she thinks everyone's on Grace's side. But there are no sides. Everyone just wants this wall between them to fall already. And it would be so easy. It's like the wall has a door, but neither of them can find the doorknob.

"Maddie, I want to ask you something, and if you don't want to answer, that's okay," I start down the rabbit hole. She narrows her eyes but doesn't speak, so I'm thinking it's my go-ahead. "You must know Grace didn't mean any disrespect to your friendship by going to that dinner. Why can't you let it go?"

"I'm not stupid, Jo. No, she didn't mean anything, but she caused me a butt load of hurt. Just think about it. She gave that woman the perfect weapon to humiliate me."

"She was stuck, Maddie. Rich was manipulating the whole thing. If she slighted him, he'd take it out on Ocean View."

"But she's so smart." Her face is a picture of derision. "How could the illustrious professor not know it would be better to tell me?"

These last words pierce me like a dart. Maybe I did nothing but get Maddie riled up again, but inside me, something churned. Who am I to step in between Grace and Maddie when I've been withholding facts from Sylvia, and now I have a sticky mess I need to clean up?

Maddie walks away from me. She takes a deep but discreet breath to steel herself, I suppose, and heads to the last cluster of women toward Grace. When she sees her, Grace's face lights up. They hug. That's a good sign. Grace introduces her to the two women she is speaking with, and after a painfully short greeting, Maddie comes to sit with us. Grace's confused stare is fixed on Maddie's back.

••

When we have all filled our plates at the lunch buffet, Fanny gathers us into the grand living room and asks everyone to tell a significant anecdote or make a comment about Grace, good or bad, a roast of sorts. One of her work friends talks about her as a teacher and tells a funny classroom story. Another speaks of having recently met Grace and how she's enjoyed working with her. Sylvia gets surprisingly emotional talking about how Grace has inspired her with her authenticity and her courage to take a new chance on love: "You did it right, girlfriend. You are an example to us all." Translation: *I envy you because I'm not able to take that leap of faith.*

The mood dips and rises by the minute, depending on what people are saying. Right after the reverential silence during Sylvia's soliloquy, we all burst out laughing when another friend, Alexandra, decides to chide Grace on her choice of music for the occasion, a playlist of forties standards, jazz romantics, and some classical music, which she finds boring. Ursula talks about the years of loyal friendship she and Grace have shared. Fanny also gets a little misty-eyed while she thanks Grace for keeping her positive and patient, and for helping her visualize her dream of being a mom during the years when she was trying to get pregnant.

I suddenly feel the need to speak.

"Laughter was the first thing that brought Grace and me together. I can't be unhappy around her. One afternoon of doing anything that strikes us as fun or funny brings perspective to my day, and my troubles seem smaller. That is why she is the one person I can't say no to."

My eyes burn. "I love her for always giving the people she cares about the benefit of the doubt. I love her because she will confront those people honestly before she gives up her trust in them." I lock eyes with Maddie, but I can't hold her icy stare. "This trait scares most of the people in her life, but I love her for it because I know how precious and rare it is for someone to give that level of loyalty."

To my surprise many in the room are sniffling, including the bride. I look at Sylvia and she turns away. Mindy and Peggy are patting me in solidarity, and a slow clapping begins and runs through the room. Maddie is silent, unmoved. A statue.

After lunch, so much wine and so many martinis have been consumed that the small clusters of women have become big circles full of laughter, delicious squealing, and feminine loudness. Some are actually singing along to the love songs. Even reluctant Alexandra is belting a sappy ballad. I'm helping two servers set the dessert table when Sylvia comes in with Fanny. Fanny is giddy and says she can't wait to dig in. I don't know if it's the wine or the sentimentality of the whole day, but I feel a sense of urgency, a need to take a bold step. They turn to leave me to my task. *Do it now.*

"Sylvia, would you stay a minute?" She hesitates for a second, and then walks back to the table. "How've you been?"

"Okay." She nods and fiddles with the cutlery.

To reveal or not to reveal, that is my question. I walk around the table and gently pull her toward a corner of the long room out of the servers' earshot.

"Right. Sylvia, I need you to trust me."

"Do you? Hard to tell."

"I don't want to give up on our friendship, but to save it we both have to give something. You have to accept my promise at face value that I haven't betrayed you, and I'll come clean. I've never lied to you, and I've been telling you, and I'm telling you again now, that nothing that's happened since Tony entered our lives should have any bearing on our friendship."

"I would like to, but I don't understand how you can say that."

"Sylvia, look at what's happened to Maddie and Grace. Rich is calling the shots there. Are we going to let that happen to us over Tony? And he's not even trying to cause trouble like Rich."

"Answer me this, Jo. Are you and Tony still seeing each other?"

"He's back in New York right now, but we do talk on a regular basis, if that's what you mean. We *are* friends."

"Wrong answer. So technically, we're exactly in the same spot we've been. I still feel you're a traitor, and you still feel you haven't done anything wrong."

"I *haven't* done anything wrong. Even if I had slept with Tony all over Miami, how does that make me a traitor? You never made a move, and you never accepted any of his advances."

"But you knew I liked him! Don't you see? Wait, what do you mean, even if you *had* slept with Tony?"

I sigh. "Sylvia, I don't want us to fight about this anymore, and this is definitely not the right time to talk about this. Do you have some time tomorrow to have tea with me?"

She looks at me suspiciously. She's about to say no.

"Please, just come over to my place tomorrow. Just come."

Despite the widespread skepticism about a bridal shower that had none of the traditional elements, the afternoon doesn't end until deep into the evening. I sense many don't want the magic of this day to end. It's not often that women can come together to sincerely celebrate each other, to have unadulterated fun with each other without an agenda of playing cheesy games, opening gag gifts, and receiving Victoria's Secret gift bags. Grace's celebration became a cathartic, bonding experience.

After a last slurred chorus of Grace's wedding song, "At Last," we begin our good-byes.

Some new friendships have been forged. I pray the magic carries forth, and some old ones can be repaired. I feel hopeful about Sylvia and me, but Maddie and Grace worry me. I don't think Maddie said more than a few words to her the entire day. Mercifully, Grace is so giddy and buzzed, I'm pretty sure she didn't notice.

•••

The orange pekoe tea sits by the perfectly arranged cannoli in expectation of Sylvia's arrival. They give the semblance of peace and agreement. I'm hoping the "Kumbaya" atmosphere will move Sylvia to put down all the slings and arrows she will probably be packing. The clock reads 5:55 p.m. She should be here any second now. Sylvia is fanatically punctual.

At 10:30 p.m., the tea is cold, the cannolis look sad, and I don't remember getting up from the couch since the sun set and the room became dark. A mixture of anger and dismay gives me the strength to get up and clean up the dainty tea service that now mocks me and makes me feel like a fool. I hate passive-aggressiveness, and in Sylvia it's become second nature. Except I was never on the receiving end.

A shy knock on my apartment door interrupts my careful placement of the cannolis back into their box. It can't be. She wouldn't dare show up this late.

"I wasn't going to come," she says at the door.

"I caught on at about seven o'clock."

We stare at each other for a few seconds, and after pointlessly waiting for an apology for the intolerable tardiness and debating whether I should say good night with a door slam, I step aside to let her in the room. She walks to the coffee table and sees the tea service. I'm no longer in a hostess mood, and besides, the tea is cold, so I won't offer it. We sit on the couch in silence. I quickly take inventory of my feelings and decide to put my indignation aside. After all, there is a purpose for this meeting, and it almost didn't happen.

"Thanks for coming."

"It seemed important to you."

"I hope it's important to you too. We've been friends for a long time and it's bizarre to me that two old bags like us can let a misunderstanding over a man ruin that."

"Old bag? Speak for yourself."

I can't help smiling. No one I know is fighting the passing years with more zeal than Sylvia, and it's working for her.

"I'm going to show you something that I should've shared with you a long time ago. You just became so insufferable about Tony and me being friendly that I held it as punishment. I hate passive-aggressive moves. They never work out the way you want."

"Oh my God, don't tell me you're going to show me an engagement ring. I'll drop dead right here in this room if you do!"

Here we go again. "Shut up and don't be ridiculous. And what if we were engaged? You have yet to coherently explain your objection to any possible relationship between Tony and me. Just say it! You want him for yourself. We're not moving any further until you admit that."

"Fine! I do. I'm nuts about the man and I hate myself for it. Especially since I turned him off so many times that he finally had enough. I pretty much gave him to you, and I can't take it. For heaven's sake, I introduced you two. I've tried to move on, but I can't. And when I see you, I know you've been with him and I ache for another chance." She whimpers so softly and miserably, it doesn't sound like Sylvia. The battle against her emotions has left her spent, and she has lost.

I take the remote control for the DVD player and press play. The image of a chef's kitchen appears on my TV and a voice off camera says, "*Jo's Kitchen* test." Sylvia shifts on the couch to face the TV.

"Join me every week and learn baking made easy. I'll teach you the secrets of the best pastry chefs around the world." After a beep, the first voice says, "Cut."

"What is that?" asks Sylvia, dabbing the tears off her cheeks with her fingers.

"Hopefully my new show on the Cooking Channel. Tony's producing it. We'll be pitching it to the network for next season."

I can see the lights go on in her head as the realization comes over her. Her eyes begin to brighten.

"This is why Tony and I have been spending time together. It was never romantic. I knew from that first lunch that he had in some way changed you, and he was always honest about being crazy for you."

"Oh God, this is all a nightmare. Ever since this man came into my life, it's not my life anymore. I don't know who I am or what I want. I want him. I don't want to want him, but I do, so much. Jo, it surprises me how much I think about him."

"Yeah, you're a mess, and I guess I didn't help much. I'm sorry I've been so harsh. I don't normally buy into chick drama, but I sure have been window-shopping lately."

Laughter interrupts Sylvia's tears.

"I should've told you, Syl, and maybe all this nonsense could've been avoided, but I was so mad that you didn't trust me."

"I told you. I've just been someone I don't even know. You're right. In all the years we've been friends, you've never given me a reason to doubt you. So, you think the show could get picked up?"

"I don't know anything about the TV business. That's all Tony. I have my hands full trying not to get too excited in case I have to face rejection."

"He must be thrilled. Producing his own show is his dream."

"He's pretty pumped, and he wanted so much to share this with you. I did too. We tried the day I surprised you in his office, but you didn't stay long enough, as I remember. And please don't be angry with Tony for not telling you. I asked him not to, and he was terrified to get in the middle.

"Jo, I'm going to ask you something. This is hard for me, but I have to. Do you think I still have a shot with him? I want to fix this. I want to give this a chance."

For so long I hoped to hear Sylvia say these words, and now I'm scared because I don't know if she's spooked Tony away forever.

"Well, if you really want it, you shouldn't worry about what could happen. Just go for it. Give it your most hellacious try and if it doesn't work, you won't live with the regret of not doing your best to turn things around because of fear. Fear has kept you captive, Sylvia. You're free now. What are you going to do about it?"

Sylvia

●

*M*e slighting Clifton made sense. Clifton slighting me is a whole different thing. *That* is incomprehensible. The walls of his tiny office seem to be closing in on me with every second that elapses. As always, I'm uncomfortable and tense, but the twitch in my eye is not severe at the moment, so I want to believe he can't see it.

"I know that we're not best friends, but I didn't expect such a cold welcome."

"Sorry to disappoint." Even when he's distant, his smile warms my world.

"Something's happened to you. You've been avoiding me, and I hate to tell you but I've invested a lot of time in this interview of yours, and you can't back out now. That's why I'm here. Is it finished or is there anything else you need from me?"

"I have no desire to back out."

"So what is it?" It alarms me that his chattiness has now become pithy speech.

"Ms. Sabatino, you are an imposing woman, indeed."

Now that's more like it. My lips curl into a bashful smile despite my efforts to control it.

He notices and chuckles. "Oh no, I don't mean in the impressive way. More like in the exhausting way."

Normally, such an observation from a male of the species would trigger a blitz of accusatory insults, ranging anywhere from *misogynistic* to *terrorist*. Instead, my heart sinks.

"You don't know me really," is the only defense I can produce.

"Sylvia, I've been alone for a very long time. I was married and divorced young, had a few moments with women here and there, but I don't play games. I don't approach a woman unless I like her, plain and simple. And I like you."

Why am I not racing out that door like greased lightning? Those last three words turn my blood into rocket fuel. *Say more things like that, please!*

"But every time I come anywhere near you, I feel the need to check myself for foul smells or an open fly because you look at me like I'm roadkill."

My warm insides are quickly cooling from the chill in my bones. "Oh, come on, you exaggerate." What I really mean is *I'm so, so sorry!*

He stares at me for a moment with a look of defeat before slumping on the edge of the desk. "It's useless. I give up."

Oh no you don't! It's now or never, Sabatino. I slowly walk over to him, lift his head up, and deposit an ever-so-soft kiss on his lips, as if asking permission to take a taste. He looks at me, searching one last time, and as he gently rises, my breasts caress his chest.

"What are you doing?" he whispers, still searching.

I coquettishly tap my finger on my slightly puckered lips and pretend to be pondering the question. "Hmm …"

"Now that's not fair." He grabs my shoulders and pushes me back a millimeter.

"What's not fair?" But I think I know exactly what he means.

"What game are you playing?"

"No game this time. Honest." We give each other knowing smiles.

He closes the millimeter gap again, and without taking his hands off my shoulders he kisses me. No asking for permission. No hesitation. A tender, lingering kiss. Then I kiss him back. And then we kiss again, harder, deeper. But now his hands are slowly traveling all around my back and his touch speaks things I've long denied wanting to hear and feel. Our kisses blend one into another, and their intensity rises with every luscious second that passes. I sense certain death will come if I stop savoring his mouth.

My blouse has become an intolerable barrier between my skin and his. He must be reading my mind, because in an instant, I feel the coolness of the room on my bare shoulders and the blissful heat of his hands on my breasts. His thumb and index finger begin a beautiful dance on my nipple, and I let out an involuntary groan.

"I'm sure glad I locked the door," he breathes in my ear, and I know he's smiling.

My eyes are closed and I'm swimming in ecstasy. "What are your intentions?" I say almost incoherently.

"My intentions are to walk you to that couch." His voice is low and velvety. *Yes, yes!*

It's all a blur, but magically I am lying on the couch, more of my skin is uncovered, and his breath warms my breasts. And then … oh merciful God, his finger barely brushes over the danger zone of my panties in progressively smaller circles. It has found the target. With a swift movement of two fingers around the fabric, I am exposed, and he lowers his mouth. I catch my breath in shock at how rapidly my desperate need for release is intensifying and suddenly, I'm fearful. My mind whispers *more, more, for heaven's sake, don't stop!* But my hands are trying to lift his head. "Tony, we shouldn't, not here," I manage to say, unconvincingly.

He looks up at me and I snap my legs closed on instinct. He's not buying it. He takes my ankles and begins to spread my legs again, tentatively. I don't fight. It's his cue. His mouth drops again and after delaying a bit by kissing my inner thigh, he knows exactly where to go. The payoff is almost immediate. Burning, consuming, unrelenting waves of heat radiate from my core, and with each wave, my body spasms. And then, even before the blissful rapture is over, he's inside me, he fills every crook and curve completely, and our hips synchronize.

Time stands still as we both surrender to the sublime rhythm of our bodies in unison. Then, I open my eyes for a fraction of a second just in time to see his blushing, moist face, eyes closed, and hear him grunt long and low, lost in ecstasy. Every cell of my body is urging me to follow him, and within seconds a powerful urgency converges in my pelvis and shakes me with an intensity of ten on the Richter scale.

We lie in silence for a while, both spent, the full weight of his warm body on mine, his heart racing, his breath blowing softly on my breasts. When we unlock our bodies, my soul screams as if split in two with a primordial ache to stay attached to him, and I'm suddenly aware of the enormous abyss in which I have lived for far too long.

••

"Ms. Sabatino, I do believe some of the things we just did are illegal in several states." His voice is a deep croak and resonates through every inch of my skin.

"A crime worth the punishment." I won't tell him I didn't even know I liked some of the things we did.

This silence. It swathes me. It loves me. It's musical and it lulls me even with the muffled sounds of the office bustle outside. My cheek feels warm near his. His arm holding me near him feels heavy and protective. How long have we been lying here? Forever would not be enough. But why is he so quiet? God, how I hate being neurotic. I'll be damned if I'm going to let my demons encroach on this moment.

"You know, I don't think I want this to be our first date. I'm going to buy you a proper dinner tomorrow, Clifton."

"Not possible. I'm going back to New York tomorrow."

The instant he utters those words my head spins, and I can't hold on to my thoughts. My memory returns to my teenage self, always giving without care for reciprocity. I watch young Sylvia, left used and discarded, yet again. My restless thoughts had settled on plans and dreams that were just conceived but a few minutes before, and already were my most precious possessions. And just like that, they are no longer mine. He's taking them with him. He's taking his squinty smile. He's taking his hands, and the heat of his skin. He'll say we'll see each other again, but the long distance will give him the perfect out. Sylvia the Woman came back to life for an hour, and now she's dead again. I miss her so.

"Boy, are you gonna miss me when I'm gone," he says.

I return from my contemplation and fix him with a stare.

"Aren't you?"

"I'm thinking," I say with my best impression of a smile.

"I'll take a rain check, okay? I'll come back down in a couple of weeks, or you can come up and see me."

"Wh-what?"

"Now don't start making excuses. I worked too hard to get you, so I'm keeping you on a tight leash."

"Won't that be hard all the way from New York?"

"For now. It's temporary. I like Miami, now even more. It shouldn't be too difficult to get transferred. I'd already thought about it when we shot the test with Jo, but now I have to factor you in the decision to relocate."

Little ol' me is a factor in a major life decision?

As if reading my mind, his blue eyes shoot daggers in my direction. "Sylvia, there's something about you that's worth coming back for, even with your smart mouth and your infernal temper."

I slap his chest with my bra before balling it up into my bag, and he laughs a bright, hearty laugh. Then I allow myself to sit back and soak in the wave of happiness all the way to my bones. Is love supposed to be such a roller coaster? A minute ago, I was preparing myself for the walk of shame. But he wants me. Even if I don't succeed in holding on to the flavor of this feeling, at this delicious moment he wants me. My body relaxes.

"Come on, you make me sound awful. I'm not that bad."

"You're joking, right? You were such a tight-ass at that first lunch with Jo, I called New York and asked the station to send someone else to do the interview."

Can you be indignant and happy at the same time? Does it matter?

I could lock my eyes on this creature for eternity, but I think it best to let him think there's a shred of reserve left in me, so I wrench myself away from him.

I pretty much skip out of the office building. On the way to the parking lot, I catch my reflection in a store window. I'm shocked and thrilled at the brazen mess that is my hair. I hope everybody can tell what I just did. And my nipples are like pencil points under my shirt. I'd better wipe this grin off my face before I get to the office. Who is that in the window? The woman looking back at me from the glass is a familiar stranger, like someone I once knew but can't quite place. Wait, I see her clearly now. Sylvia the Woman is back all grown up, maybe for good.

•••

*T*ony. Tony whose voice grated on me from our very first phone call. Tony whose overconfident and persistent advances I rejected with implacability. Tony who in the span of three months has done what others have tried for years, and miraculously awakened a part of me that I thought was condemned to eternal slumber.

I'm so exhausted, but in a good way. Tony left yesterday and I haven't stopped thinking about him since our time together in his office, and thinking hard. I keep mentally injecting Tony into every aspect of my life, and it all looks so rich and bright now. Shopping, cooking dinner, daydreaming about him in the middle of a conference, it all plays like an adventure in my head. I'm trying not to get excited and let my imagination revamp my entire life with the insertion of romance, but I'm not having much success. I feel a twinge of remorse when I think of how vocal I've been about a woman not needing a man to be happy. I spent so much time pontificating about women needing to find totality in themselves. Not that I've changed my mind about that, but I can't deny that my new fullness of being has a whole lot to do with Tony.

I wonder if Grace will be able to tell that something is different. Listen to me, I sound like a teenager who just lost her virginity. What I really wonder is if I'll tell her. It's going to be fun shopping with Grace for her bridal intimates. The lingerie department will have a whole new hue for me now.

On a cooler day, I would choose a table on the terrace at Mariposa, but this sticky September afternoon is screaming for the air-conditioned seating inside the mall. After we order Grace's crab cake and my Tuscan chicken melt, we settle into comfortable conversation about the wedding and the fundraiser. Grace is in a permanent state of euphoria while catching me up on all the wedding preparations. I notice she's pecking at the breadbasket like a hungry chicken.

"Grace, ease up. All that bread's going to stick out of your dress."

"It's stress-eating. I hope my nerves will keep me from eating a few days before the wedding to make up for all this munching."

"Here, take some of my vegetables instead of all that bread."

"Not unless you're putting some chocolate sauce on them. I'll make you a deal. I'll have the sweet potato flan for dessert. Sweet potatoes are vegetables, right? And they're comforting. Good for the jitters."

She looks determined, so I'll get off her back. At least we'll be shopping and walking it off. She's very brave to go looking for honeymoon lingerie after this lunch.

My anxiety returns when we leave the restaurant. When the pace slows, it will be impossible for me not to tell my tasty secret. I'm on sensory overload. Streams of people flow through the mall walkways under the bright glass dome. Browsers shuffle from window to window, slowing down traffic for the ones power-walking toward a specific destination with laser focus. The kiosk vendors step into the flow with unabashed determination to hawk their goods. Children's bellows stand out from the natural hum of the bustling crowd. The sound of scanning registers and the monotone "have-a-nice-day" from the cashiers repeat against a background of large screens and wall-to-wall posters with enticing ads.

For all my preparation and distraction, everything spills out as from a fired machine gun.

"I know it's a far cry from the Yankees T-shirt I'm used to wearing to bed," Grace says, "but I was thinking of getting something slutty but romantic for the honeymoon. No thong panties though. Butts the size of mine have no business fooling with rump floss. Whaddaya think, Syl? You're the expert."

In my paranoia, I mistake her wide-eyed, vivid grin for provocation.

"How am I the expert on being slutty? I've been out of the sex loop for a very long time, you know? Sorry, but I've been a little too busy publishing a magazine to get my slutty on, but I'll tell you what: If I did, it would be more than justified because lord knows I'm overdue." My response is frenetic.

"Hey, hey, hey, where did that come from? I just meant you're the *style* expert. Get a grip! What is up with you?"

I look down hating myself. When my eyes meet hers, I see the look of understanding in her face.

"Omigod, did you and Tony …? Sylvia, you did! Omigod, when? How?"

What the hell. And so I tell her everything, not the during but the before and the after. I tell her about how foolish I felt after Jo's revelation, about how I marshalled every ounce of zeal I could find within me and practically seduced Tony. And I told her I could no longer recognize myself.

"Can I get a hallelujah!" Grace raises her hands in reverence.

"I'm scared, Grace. I like him a lot. I don't want to screw this up."

"I like him too, Syl, because anyone that can bring out all this vulnerability from inside you has to be a good guy. This feels different, Sylvia. This time it's a man who cares about you and can't wait to come back to you. So what if it's long-distance? Do you know how many women our age wish they had someone who cared enough to fight with them and for them? Who cares if he's on Mars!"

She's right, as usual. Her excitement is making me giddy again.

"Shoo away the fears. They're nothing but leftover demons from the past. The universe will always assist if you follow your path audaciously, my friend."

"From what profound work of literature did you get that, Grace?"

"A fortune cookie."

Peggy

•

I didn't want to come. I fought it as long as I could. If it works, I may finally figure out the mystery and make some solid plans. But if it doesn't …

Whatever. No guts, no glory. I'm fully aware that this holy war between Penny and me is the only possible explanation for my decision to come here. I project my own self-loathing onto my sister. I allow her to make me feel insignificant. That last argument was the worst we've had in years. When we hung up, I was spent, but now there is an anxious residue, an urge to leap into action in some radical way that will shake me out of this life of doldrums. Like a snake out of old skin.

And so here I am. I want to help Mackenzie, but I must know what his situation is. He likes me and trusts me to a degree, but he keeps me at arm's length, and I can't do anything of significance for him long-distance. But what makes me think my intervention would be wanted? I didn't even have a clear idea of my intentions when I decided to come here, or of my desired outcome.

My heart is racing. The surroundings do nothing to soothe my nerves. I haven't been to this part of Homestead too often, but I never thought of it as being an unsavory area of town. I skip over several broken steps on my way up to the third floor. Every wall is smeared with mildew, and many are dotted with holes. Bullet holes?

I'm tired of waiting on ideal circumstances to live my life, to follow my heart, but the sight that greets me when I reach the door makes me regret this decision instantly.

The door to the apartment is open. The frame is so warped, the door refuses to fit. Just as I'm about to knock, I hear loud thwacks and muffled cries. I don't knock. I push the door and the scene inside takes shape. In a subconscious gesture of disgust my nose wrinkles and I jerk my head backward. I feel the blood drain from my face. In a mere moment, all my childhood memories lie tangled and soiled, disfigured and grotesque.

The belt comes down over the boy, and his knees bend to the ground. The leather hits him again, this time on the right side of his rib cage and leaves a fiery red welt on his bare torso. Then the belt comes down again and again in what seems like unending hell.

"Mama!" The cry of a child in pain, a child wrenched from his very core.

My only reason to live at this moment is to stop her, to hurt her, to save him.

"You will do what I tell you, boy." The slurred speech of intoxication. The belt whips again, and Mac raises his hand to shield his face. The belt descends on his forearm. Mac winces and as he closes his eyes, he doesn't see the belt come down yet again over his head.

"No, Mama, no!"

I hear myself scream. In an instant, I grab the woman by the T-shirt, and shove her away from the boy. My hands encircle her neck as I pin her to the wall. I can never let go. She must forever remain far away from the boy. The image of the welt on his skin flashes in my brain, and my fingers tighten. Her liquored breath burns my eyes. My sister's words of derision ring in my ears. My mother's look of perpetual disappointment washes over me, and I squeeze harder. The woman's eyes bulge with astonishment and fear, or maybe because I am squeezing her eyeballs out. My face is wet with warm tears.

"Ms. Paulson, stop it, back away, don't do this. Let go of her!" Mac screams in my ear and pulls at my arms, but my fingers won't let go. But now, I want to let go, I think.

"Ms. Paulson, you ain't helping, please, please let her go." The desperation in his plea jolts me, and I release her instantly, as if her skin scorched mine.

She coughs and gags, and her eyes are hot pokers that brand me with the heat of my current reality. My villainy comes into focus. I back toward the opposite wall, putting distance between me and my deed. When my back feels the old concrete, I slide down until I hit the floor in a sobbing heap.

"You're going to *jaaail* … this here is *MYYYYY* son … *nochurrrbusiness* … calling the cops … you'll be sorry … don't give a damn who you are …" Her words drop from her mouth in nearly unintelligible phrases.

She yells, curses, threatens in a raspy, injured voice. I hear her, but I can't look at her. I push my eyes into the balls of my hands so hard, I feel dizzy and see stars. I feel a firm pull on my elbow and I rise.

"Get out, just get out!" Mackenzie shoves me out into the hallway and slams the door hard. The embarrassment and misery in his tear-streaked face will be etched in my memory forever.

"You little piece of trash! I'm your mother! Who is that? Why's she in our business?"

I bend over the railing in the hallway and just about upchuck, so I lean back against the wall. I hear her on the phone calling the police. I guess I should call someone too.

Grace.

I had to insist that she didn't bring Jack because I didn't think I could face him, so I forgave her when she showed up at the police station with Mindy. In fact, it made sense. It hadn't occurred to me that other than keeping me company, there wasn't much else Grace could do to help the situation.

Mindy got to work immediately. Besides the fact that I know nothing about law enforcement, the whole afternoon was nothing but a blurry nightmare. I spent an hour talking to the cops. I told them about my relationship with Mac, what I saw when I arrived at the apartment, and as much as I could remember about what I did to the woman. Bail was set at $1,000, which seemed strangely low, but I thought maybe Mindy had something to do with that. I do remember her breathing deeply when she came to where Grace and I were sitting. She was flushed and sounded like she had been doing hard physical labor, like digging in a mine. Digging me out of my grave, more like it. She told us that she was fairly certain that I would be charged with a battery misdemeanor and something about the cops being willing to overlook the strangulation portion of the attack, I can't remember why. It sounded morbidly funny to me. The arraignment will be in three weeks, and I'm temporarily suspended from work pending the outcome. The clock has stopped on my life until then.

••

I keep reminding myself to be grateful, that I got off easy. That the worst is over, that good things will come out of this mess. It's all true, but I'm not there yet.

It's been four weeks since that dreadful day and one week since the arraignment. Mindy called in a favor from a friendly judge and got me off without one single day in jail. I don't know, but considering my actions, that can be nothing short of a miracle. In a twisted way, some things worked out okay. Others seem laughable. The judge put me in a first offense diversion program, which apparently is a big name for community service. The absurd part is that I have to take anger management classes. Me. Anger management classes. I can't decide if it's more embarrassing or ridiculous.

I shouldn't scoff. What I did was reprehensible, no matter what my intentions. I try not to speculate about what my friends and my colleagues must be thinking about me, not to mention Mackenzie. I wanted to support him, and instead I let him down. In the grand scheme, putting some hours in at an old folks' home and taking some classes is nothing in comparison to my relentless self-loathing. Regardless, the cops' investigation, and the fact that my actions were deemed "in defense of others," got the charges reduced to simple assault.

The jaw-dropper though, was that this whole pile of filth may end up being the fastest way to get Mackenzie a college scholarship. The cops filed a report with the Department of Children and Families, and last I heard, Mac was placed in a foster home for a year until he turns eighteen. In the meantime, he'll be looking into some programs that help kids get scholarships.

Yes, I am grateful and humbled, but today will not be pleasant. I'm torn between wanting to get this over with and not wanting to face it at all. Like dental work. I'm so ashamed.

I see Jack's car through the raindrops that mottle the window. I guess it's time. I open the door before they ring. Grace hugs me tight and kisses me. Jack hugs me too. He must be so uncomfortable. I wonder how much of this is his own willingness to help and not Grace's cajoling.

"Are you ready?" Right to the point. He wants to get this done too.

"I better be."

"It's going to be fine, Peggy. The worst is over." Grace lovingly arranges my hair around my face.

"I know. I'm grateful that I'm not in jail, but honestly, I'm so afraid of losing my job."

"Maybe you won't. You don't know what they're going to say." Jack's intentions are good, but he doesn't sound too convinced himself.

"Come on, Jack. The college board of trustees summons me to come see them—what was it the letter said? —'as soon as the legal process is completed and before you resume your coaching schedule.' Do you think they're throwing me a welcome-back party? I'd bet on a proper dismissal."

He looks at his shoes. He knows I'm right.

Suddenly I feel like all the air in my lungs has escaped. I plop into an armchair. "Give me a minute." I take a few deep breaths. "Right now, my biggest concern is not fainting when I walk into that room alone."

"You won't be alone. I'll walk in with you," Jack says.

"What? Can you do that?"

"Jack asked them. He told them your present emotional state should be taken into consideration, and that you wouldn't mind if he were present to hear what they had to say."

"And they were okay with that?"

"Of course. I've sat in on other matters." Jack's lips turn into a playful grin. "Remember when you were first hired? Besides, they listen to me. You know I'm a delight."

It's the first time I've laughed since I walked into Mackenzie's place. My eyes burn with trapped tears, but in gratitude, the least I can do for this man is spare him a scene.

This tiny bit of lightheartedness and the knowledge that I won't have to walk in alone gives me enough courage to leave the apartment. I did not anticipate that the wave of fear would return as soon as I walked out of the building. The prospect of getting into Jack's car takes me back to the ride to the police station in back of the patrol car. I find it hard to get in, but the skies rip open, and the abrupt and unforgiving sheet of rain soaks me with every condemning drop.

•••

When did I first notice that I was getting old? Easy. It was the day I heard songs from my twenties and thirties on the oldies radio station. It was an aha moment, but not the good kind. A sense of urgency came over me. But even then, there was no reconciliation between that realization and my desire to live life at full throttle. My head felt the onrush of age, but my heart still felt vigorous and curious and open to every possibility.

Lately though, it's all coming undone. Life is leaking out of me. I strain to hold on to all that is good, and I fail. The only thing injecting life into me is this small, muddy square of a window in the vestibule outside the conference room, just big enough to allow me a glimpse of the sun in relentless battle to break through the thickness covering the sky. I'd bet the sun will lose and yet, every second the battle wears on, the sky lightens a speck.

After a final hug and a few quick words to uplift me, Grace heads to her office. Jack is checking emails on his phone, and I'm sure he's glad not to engage in endless speculation about what awaits behind that door. I sit here, my eyes following each raindrop sliding down the murky window, waiting to be called in, going back and forth between regretting ever going to that apartment and being glad that I was there to stop the walloping. It took me so long to muster the courage to go there. I was so afraid of destroying my fragile relationship with Mac if I poked my nose into his home life, but I convinced myself that perdition lies in all the decisions not made for fear. And now here I am, feeling as if my life isn't mine anymore.

I did not get fired. I got praised. I got a promise that Mackenzie would get a full scholarship to play tennis for the college. For a kid who hasn't caught many breaks in life, they're all piling up now. Even stoic Jack couldn't hide his relief when we got out of the conference room. He called Grace right away, his voice bordering on giddy.

As soon as it was all settled, when I found a soft place to land after being in a holding pattern for an eternity, I made my first executive decision, and showed up at Penny's in Virginia unannounced.

For the first time, I'm aware of the compulsory silence in the suburban cul-de-sac where her house sits. I hear birds chirping. I don't remember the last time I heard birds near my home. The endless chain of white picket fences, the cookie-cutter homes, only distinguishable by a flower box here, a flag there, a rocking chair on the porch.

"Margaret! What are you doing here?"

I pushed into the house gently before I answered. "I came to get those pearls. The wedding is next weekend."

"You should've called first."

"No, Penny. If I'd called first, I wouldn't be standing here right now. You would've found a way to pick another fight with me to keep me from coming. I'm done with that."

"I don't know that we have a lot to say to each other."

"Are you joking? We have a whole lifetime of stuff to talk about, and it's gonna happen now. I'm not leaving until I say what I came to say. And I want those pearls."

Penny exhales in irritation and rolls her eyes just like she did when we were teenagers. For some reason, that's comforting. Sisters reverting to what we used to be when we were children. Then, she refocuses and shoots me her standard icy stare. Once again, Penny's eyes are the cracked mirror that reflect a distorted image of what I am. I don't want to look at that image any longer.

I wait for an invitation to move farther in than the door frame, but since it doesn't look like I'll get one, I walk in unsolicited and sit on the couch. She's still by the door.

"Where does pathetic and meek Margaret get the courage to just show up somewhere uninvited?"

"Quit it. Stop spitting your poison at me to make yourself feel better. You're miserable. I don't know why, but you are, and I'm tired of being your punching bag."

"Keep your voice down. My grandkids are upstairs." She inches toward me, her arms crossed. "And you're wrong. I'm not the one who's miserable. You keep trying to push yourself on me and my family because you're lonely, but that's not my fault. You made your life choices. Leave me alone and move on."

"Aunt Peggy!" The kids thunder down the stairs and tackle me deep into the couch.

"Leave Aunt Peggy be, kids. Did y'all finish your homework?" Every word Penny speaks to the kids is laced with aggravation.

"That's okay. I have some presents for you." From my duffle bag, I pull a stylish sky-blue purse for Patricia and a video game for Chester, and they both thank me with a hug. Penny is seething. "Okay, I'll tell you what. After dinner, we can catch up. Run along and let me talk to Granny."

"What makes you think you're staying for dinner?" Penny whispers as her eyes follow the disappearing children up the stairs.

"I'm staying until you and I come to a place where we can behave like adult sisters. I always believed you when you told me you were better than I was, you made better choices, that I had a lousy life and that's why I was always trying to visit and mix with your family. But now I realize you've been trying to keep me far away because you don't want me to see how miserable you are."

"Shut up! You're crazy. I wouldn't change a thing about my life. I have a home, a husband, and a family. It's what I always wanted, and I got it." Her voice rises as if she can't hear well enough to convince herself.

"But you have no identity, Penny. God bless, you were more of a person when you were working for the chiropractor and hanging out with your friends at the clubs. At least those were your choices."

"Shut up, just SHUT UP! You know nothing about me."

"I know it's not even noon and you smell of whiskey. That tells me enough."

She covers her face with her hands and cries the sobs of a little girl. She growls in anger into her hands; the edges of her face where her hairline begins turn crimson. She flops on the loveseat and cries in desperation. I come to her and she turns away from me, but when I insist, she surrenders and cries on my shoulder even harder. I rock her in silence.

After a long purging, she wipes her blotchy face with the corner of her robe.

"I've become my grandchildren's hired help. I haven't worn anything but robes and muumuus in months. Charlie and I haven't had sex in years." At this, she looks at me pleadingly.

"I'm so sorry, Penny. I really am. I know what it's like to think you have the life you want, and have it turn in a different direction without your permission."

"No, you don't." Her shoulders slumped, she gets up and walks to the kitchen table to get a napkin and wipes her nose. "Your life is exactly what you want it to be, and I've hated you all my life for having the guts to go after it. I don't know when mine got away from me. Somewhere I lost control. You have no idea what it's like to wake up every day wondering where life is going to take you instead of steering it yourself."

"Oh really? Is that what you think? Let's order some pizza for dinner, and I'll tell you about my life lately. It'll make you cringe." I chuckle dejectedly. "Penny, I don't expect that we will ever be loving sisters. We're too old now to create a brand-new relationship, but whether we like it or not, there's a bond that pulls us together, and up until now, we've done nothing but stretch that bond and pull at it, trying to break it. We have to stop. You hurt me, a lot. And I can hurt you too, but I want to stop."

"I'm no whore, you know?"

"I'm not a lesbian."

"Why weren't we closer, Margaret?"

"When we were young, we were very different. Now, I don't know. I don't think you like talking to me."

"Nuh-uh. The opposite. Every time I talk to you or see you, I want to run out of here, be independent, do me. But I can't, and it does no one any good for me to have those feelings, you know?"

I do. It is as I always suspected. We've been busy begrudging each other our choices. She's missed having time for herself, and at times I've wanted the constant company of live bodies around me.

"I understand. Thanks for having the courage to tell me. This is the first time I can remember not feeling like a disappointment to my family. You're the only family I have, Penny."

"Mom wasn't disappointed in you, Peggy. You were just smarter than her and she didn't get you." She sighs deeply and slides back into the loveseat. "And if I'm going to be completely honest, I was jealous of your relationship with Dad. Every time you two went on one of your walks, I cried."

"He worried about you, Penny. It unnerved him that you were so boy crazy, but Mom swallowed him up when he asked her to stop encouraging you. I suspect he felt guilty about not being more assertive with her."

I have a choice. I can go home with the knowledge that I wasn't as undesirable to my family as I thought and try to love myself more for the second half of my life, or I can use it to forge a long-overdue bond with my sister. Why not both?

"I'll tell you what. How about we try to be each other's support and let Mom and Dad rest?" I put my arm around her, and the little girl I knew long ago appears again and puts her head on my shoulder. I feel her exhale the weight of decades.

"Now where are my pearls?"

"In the attic. There's squirrels in there. They freak me out."

Always so prissy. "We'll go together."

Grace

•

My first sight as this day dawns is a sky blushed pink and caramel over the silvery bay waters of Key Largo. A lonely fishing boat glides from the pier, cutting a gash into the glassy surface. A woodpecker dots the silence with its insistent assault on a tree trunk. And for accompaniment, the soft purr of sleep coming from the man lying next to me. The man who will be my husband when the sun ends the cycle it has just begun.

One fleeting moment, a variation detected in the cadence of a familiar voice, can alter your reality and veer your journey in the opposite direction. That is what happened. That's why I'm here. This is my day. Of all the days of my life, God made this one just for me.

Jack was an unexpected gift when he arrived. I wasn't looking for love because other women's anecdotes about dating and marriage at our age left me exhausted and grateful to be done with all that. Oh, I dated, but sporadically and systematically. It was my way of staying connected but unattached. Dates were a free meal, an opportunity to dress up, and, on a lucky day, for interesting company.

And if love had become foreign, marriage was but a misty memory that others had to endure but would never touch me again. Jack's presence didn't change my stance on commitment. He was a lovely complement to my already rich life full of travel, raising a teenage daughter, and ownership of every decision made, wise or foolish.

In those early days of courting, Jack would say, "I'm drawn to obsession by your independence. I'm always aware that every day I'm with you is because you want me, not because you need me." There's a lesson for every woman age 15 to 105.

Six months into our fragile relationship, rumblings about marriage came from Jack. I fended off the hints casually.

"Marriage is so irrelevant for people like us. We've both done it. We suck at it. Who needs it? Why can't we just shack up? We're too old to care what people think."

Then it all changed.

"Grace, I wouldn't've hung around this long if I didn't believe we were on the path to marriage somewhere down the line. I love you. I want to marry you, but if you don't feel the same way, then it's best to talk about it now."

That was it. This was not the sweet, indulging voice I had come to know. It sounded deliberate and determined. In that instant, I knew I didn't want to be this man's girlfriend forever. This was a man you married. I wanted to be his wife.

It still took us four years to get here, but now it was love with a purpose. Every moment together was a lesson in each other as individuals and as a couple, every experience a building block for our future union that would not include the mistakes of the past.

"The ceremony has to start at six o'clock sharp. Pictures have to start at six forty-five so we can catch the sunset as it changes colors." Fanny is issuing edicts as she debriefs us on her timetable.

At three o'clock, makeup and hair. At five, Jack is fully dressed and posing for his groom pictures on the balcony of our suite and in its elegant living room. They leave to shoot around the tropical grounds of the hotel, and the girls are left with me to complete the holiest of wedding-day tasks: dressing the bride.

As Mindy and Jo spoon me into the dress, not without significant effort, the vision begins to take form. The gauzy layers of chiffon embrace the contours of my body as if they had found their long-lost home. When they start on the clasps, I take a deep breath, knowing I may not be able to exhale until I take it off, but I can't have it both ways: I can look good or I can breathe. Mindy, Jo, and Fanny stare at me as if in the presence of a spirit. After the horror of the first fitting, the magical elves they call seamstresses at the bridal salon turned limp fabric into a miracle.

"You know, come to think of it, I should've had a bigger wedding," I gush at my reflection.

"Of course, why wouldn't you, since you handled planning this one so well?" Fanny breaks the spell with a sarcastic roll of her eyes and gets us back to business. The last twenty minutes before the ceremony go by in a blur of pre-wedding pictures and last-minute instructions from my fussy self-appointed wedding planner.

Finally, it's time. Jack walks into the foyer of the suite for his first look. The girls exit the room quietly to allow us the full intimacy of this moment. This is probably the most nervous I've been through the entire planning madness. He stops a few inches away, he catches his breath, he smiles, and then he kisses me.

"I'm sorry. Maybe I should've made sure no one was here for this." My voice shakes.

"Nothing and no one could ruin this moment. It's perfect. You're perfect."

We walk down wide stairs arm in arm. This is totality. I am bathed in the magic of the moment and the surroundings, and

I am determined to remain aware of it all. I've been in this place many times since we chose it as our venue, but now the scenery overwhelms me — the fanciful complexion of the sky with its promise of orange and violet and sepia soon to come, the compact crescent of the tide line washed in sandy gold, salmon-pink tinsel over the blue-green cove.

Ahead, the holy place where God will consecrate this life-changing alliance beckons, a rustic wooden platform bedecked in gold ribbons and red and white flowers. To my left, the cheerful flickering tiki torches illuminate smiling faces and shapes that are familiar, but at this moment indistinct. Jack's warmth on my skin is all I feel, his body next to mine is all I see. To my right, a bright flash of fiery red fabric interrupts my trance. Jack notices that I stop and tenderly urges me on. The red phantom becomes solid and plants a hard kiss on my cheek. It's Lily.

Love is a willful choice to make or not, but care must be taken. Love is not, as we believe in our tender youth, a lucky strike from a mystical cosmos. The weight of my choice confronts me when I turn to look at Jack as the ceremony begins. If I allowed it, I could faint, but I'm determined to take in every moment. This will not be just a blur in my memory. The pastor speaks of the ancient significance of this ritual, our coming together by divine orchestration with friends and family, the witnesses to this moment, to proclaim our covenant.

Surprisingly, it resonates in the deepest recesses of my soul. At no other moment in my life have I felt such alignment with spirit.

••

I'm married. Just like that. An hour ago, I had been single for fourteen years, and now I'm Mrs. Masters under the laws of God and man. The pictures have been taken, and our friends await to greet us for the first time as husband and wife. Cheers erupt as we enter the sweeping two-level terrace. An elegant long table dressed in white linen is bursting with speckled red and gold rose petals, like debris left from the colorful explosion of the dramatic flower arrangements placed as centerpieces. Glass and silver twinkle when touched by twilight and the endless row of candles.

The tropical forest on which the high open balcony is perched is dense and untamed. Swaying palm fronds and leaves create shadowy figures against an ardent red sky as light gives way to dark. The long terrace commands a view over the wilderness into the tops of the trees and, beyond, the boundless, sleepy sea. Its aroma, the rustling of the palms below, the ringing of festive voices, the clinking of toasting glasses, all captivate me. The warmth of contentment and the perfume of joy intoxicate me.

I steal a moment to engrave the scene in my memory. Jack seems bigger than life from where I stand, his shoulders even more geometric. He's in a huddle with the men, and I hear the boom of collective male laughter. He turns for an instant and his eyes search for me. He flashes a smile laden with a thick mix of joy, love, and lust. A tremor travels through me. How silly. After all these years.

A gaggle of women including Lily and to my astonishment, Maddie standing at a certain distance with Sylvia and Peggy, break my trance with congratulatory hugs and squeals and escort me to the table. The sight of Maddie armed with a drink brings back memories of the banquet, and I shiver a little. I see a troupe of servers approach with large trays. It's time to surrender to the revelry that will make this the most important day on every calendar for the rest of my life.

The retired sun has left an indigo sky with random gray brushstrokes for clouds. The gray dissolves into twinkling stars. Lily and I sit on wicker chairs watching the heavenly show in comfortable silence, a first in a long time. I look in the near distance at the long table and I see my friends lazily savoring second helpings of Jo's fantastic orange blossom Grand Marnier wedding cake and sipping lattes. My own joy is reflected in every single face.

"I climbed a mountain, Mom, an actual mountain. It was the most exhilarating thing I've ever done. And when I reached the top, I had the strangest feeling. It was as if I had just been introduced to myself. I know, it sounds weird. I don't know how to explain it. I've never pushed myself that hard to do anything in my life. I didn't even want to do it, but once I got started, I knew that I wouldn't quit unless I dropped dead. I feel different since that day."

There's been a shift in Lily. She's shedding her old skin, her complacency, her compulsion to drift through life. She's ready to push herself.

"I'm sorry, Mom. I'm sorry for running away from you because the voice in my own head that said I can't do anything right sounded like you."

I assess her words with a mixture of confusion and sadness. "I'll never win any mother-of-the-year awards, but have I ever said you can't do anything right?"

"No." She sighs after pondering the question. "The opposite, actually."

"Then the voice in your head sounds like you, not me," I say, not unkindly.

She lunges and embraces me so hard it hurts, in the best of ways.

"I met a girl in Santa Barbara that runs a small home goods store and she asked if I could help her on weekends during the holidays. I'm going to take the job and save the extra money so

I can go back to school in January and take one or two courses."

This moment, right now, in this place, listening to these words, is the closest my life will ever come to being perfect.

The guests are gone, the lights in our hotel room are dim, the air permeated with the smell of our freshly bathed bodies. I come to bed and find my husband under the covers, his torso exposed, his eyes closed. I lie next to him and exhale deeply. I'm a married lady. I look out the panoramic window and stare at the starry sky and the glistening surface of the ocean. I want to make a mental imprint of this moment as the happiest day of my life fades into history. I submit to it, swathe myself in its perfection. Jack turns on his side and faces me. He caresses my arm and smiles.

"Are you tired?" he says softly.

"No, happy."

His smile widens, he comes closer and kisses me.

"I'm also nervous." I giggle a little.

"Why?" He is genuinely surprised.

"Will it be different now? *Should* it be different now?"

He knows exactly what I mean. "It should and it will be different. And better."

Her hands trace his face, and her eyes invite him. His body delivers its complete weight on her and she feels the familiar hardness of his body, his arms, his thighs, all of it. He kisses her neck just below her earlobe; he nuzzles the same spot and kisses it again. His warm hand travels under her silken robe and finds the space under her breast, and as his fingers brush her skin, her body collapses to receive his. He thanks her with a deep, deliberate, and demanding kiss. Her desire mounts and she places her hands over his bare chest as if she could stop the inevitable or slow its rushing advance. His heart beats wildly under her palms. It won't be long now. Their bodies celebrate together and give wings to swelling passion burning with the fire of long nurtured anticipation.

Then, a temporary peace descends upon them. His head rests on the space between her breasts; his eyes are closed as he steadies his breathing. He runs his hands up and down the landscape of her body from her hips to the soft edges of her breasts, and she trembles from within. He raises his head to kiss her shoulder, the hollow of her neck, the side of her breast. She groans. His body shifts over her and she feels his muscles harden. It begins again. A dance done thousands of times before is, indeed, suddenly new.

He was right. It was different. At times, I seemed to be outside my body and watching us, indulging in delicious voyeurism, every touch felt, every kiss savored, every sound an urgent plea to never stop. No detail missed.

I watch Jack sleep deeply and peacefully, but I can't. I'm unwilling to let go of this day and if I sleep, morning will come. I visually trace every inch of his skin that is not covered by sheets, and the memory of what I don't see and of our wedding night lovemaking awakens my body in spite of my exhaustion. Yes, he was right when he said it would be better. *Better* doesn't do it justice.

•••

*B*ags are packed, passports and plane tickets in order. Tomorrow at this time, we will be in Rome to start a proper honeymoon. Two weeks traveling through Italy, another dream coming true.

It's been a week since the wedding, and life gets richer by the minute. Routine will set in inevitably, and we'll have to be ever vigilant to keep us fresh and engaged as all couples must or should. The road has been so long and so often obstructed, that I also know there won't be a day that I'm not grateful for this gift, this new breath of life.

My greatest wedding present by far had to be Lily. Not just her unexpected presence, but her reinvention. I often wondered whether she would ever be able to sidestep the drama of her childhood. I'd like to think at some point in our lives we disentangle ourselves from the brambles of our early years and clear a new path, but some do so late, like me. And some never do. For a while I feared my only child would be one of those who would forever tumble in the mire of timeworn anger. But I see now that she wants to be free, and the same tenacity she once used to push against me, she will now use to break free.

And then there's Maddie. All adults have that molecule of childlike innocence that allows them to think from time to time that some adversities will just go away, that things will get better all by themselves. When I saw Maddie at the shower and at the wedding, my first thought was one of naïve elation. *She came.* We didn't communicate in any way after the banquet, so I had no reason to think she would show up to either event, but seeing her there gave me every hope that our trouble would pass. Of course, it's not that easy, is it?

"My name is on the order for the flowers," she explained at the wedding. "Fanny wanted me to be here when they arrived. Besides I'm the preacher's ride. I do want you to know that I wish you all the best, Grace. You deserve it. No matter what, I'm truly happy for you."

I didn't believe her. Fanny was perfectly capable of solving the flower situation, and the preacher could've found his way. The finality of her tone ran through my body like an electric charge.

Something has gone terribly wrong. There is a crack in the foundation of what I thought was our friendship, a deep fracture, and all the king's horses and all the king's men can't put us back together again.

I'm left with the fury in her eyes as she spoke her measured and icy words at the wedding, with the regret of having wounded her by not telling her about that wretched dinner with Rich. As an act of contrition, I wrote her a long email three days ago beseeching her to forgive me for not grasping the enormity of my offense in her eyes. I proposed that we try to create a new definition for our relationship as long as it could still exist in some form. I hoped that she would allow us to recover whatever vestiges of our friendship remained and rebuild for the sake of what it once was. I said my trip would give her time to think it all through, but I begged for confirmation before I left, at least, that she would consider my pleas. As of this moment, no acknowledgement has arrived.

I grieve for the loss of Maddie as I would a death, but I'm not surprised. Most of my friendships have had an expiration date.

Looking back at the five months since my engagement, I'm astonished to revisit the twists and turns in the lives of my friends. Like the phoenix, they have burned to ashes and risen to become purified versions of themselves. Each one has broken the chains that held her captive in her own unique world, and stepped into life with a new outlook, her burdens abandoned. And as for me, I see that my life has even more definition and a fresh authenticity to it. A richer journey begins now.

The takeaway is this: turning points in someone's path don't come only once or twice. Any given day can bring new awareness and opportunities for new beginnings, some that change life radically, for better or worse. Life does grant do-overs, you just have to position yourself for a good one. And while on the path, be prepared for some relationships to turn poisonous. The good news is that having at least some genuine friends can be a powerful antidote.

Women throughout the ages, scholars, dilettantes, and fools, have argued about the who, the why, and the how of our deliverance. I, for one, have recently learned that all avenues are acceptable. It's okay to let someone be your hero. We may even be called upon to be heroic and rescue someone else, or best of all, we can rescue ourselves and become our own heroes.

Epilogue

My husband. It's been a little over a year since our wedding day, and I am still filled with wonder as I lie here in our bed watching Jack sleep and knowing that he is my husband, all mine.

I am keenly aware that it is not advisable to rely heavily on another human for direction, but in Jack I have found order and constancy. He takes the shards of my life, turns them into recognizable pieces, and puts them together so that it all makes perfectly beautiful sense.

My love stirs. "You're awake before me." His words are thick with sleepy surprise.

"I couldn't go back to sleep. Besides I like to watch you and I don't get many chances."

"Are you ready for coffee?"

"If you are."

"Me? Always ready for coffee." He stretches his long body, and his arms land around me. He covers my face in kisses, and promptly rises to perform the task of fixing our first cups of coffee, as he does every weekend morning. I could lounge eternally in bed, swaddled in the warmth of our sheets and his smell on the pillow. I noticed early on in our relationship that Jack always smelled like sweet rolls baking in the oven. I'm sure it's just my perception, but it certainly adds to the feeling of comfort and safety he gives me.

But I fear if I don't get moving, my morning will vanish in delicious idleness. I pull out some white-and-silver wrapping paper from the closet and torpidly carry the heavy gift box to the bed. It's hard to believe I'm wrapping a large sunflower-yellow Dutch oven as a bridal shower gift for Sylvia, of all people. Not only because Sylvia was the last of the group I thought would ever get married again, but also because she's on this new homemaking kick. She asked all her friends to help her equip her kitchen, which up to now has served only as wine storage.

As I fold the shimmery paper around the box in tight angles, I meditate on how my friends seem to have hit their strides in the past year, how it started with our wedding and now it's come full circle with Sylvia and Tony preparing for theirs. No two people I've ever met seem more suited for each other. Even Jack and I seem dissonant next to those two, and that's saying something.

Tony has another woman who worships him besides Sylvia. After all, he made her a celebrity. Yes, big, brash Jo is a cooking maven on TV. She even gets recognized in public sometimes. It's happened twice while I've been with her, and I love to stand back and watch her sign autographs and take selfies with her fans.

"I'm no Rachael Ray, you know?" she often says with humility, but I can tell she's never felt more gratified by her work. And so she should.

Peggy's darkest days are also over. She says she'll never be able to stop the shakes every time she thinks of that awful day when she was arrested, but time is forgiving even if we're not. She is now in charge of athletic and specialty scholarships at our college. Mackenzie is ranked number three in college tennis for the entire state and doing quite well with his academics. Peggy can spot talent, no question.

The greatest U-turn has to be Maddie's. Our relationship is all but dead. We often coincide in social gatherings, and we're civil to each other, but she dropped out of our foodie group. Nonetheless, the other women keep me informed about her. Not only is she swimming in money from her divorce settlement, but after the initial funds raised at the banquet were depleted in addressing the urgent repairs to the infrastructure, she used her own money to turn the Ocean View Community Center into a leading social service provider in the city. Other similar independent centers have popped up in several neighborhoods in the span of a few months, and they all come to *the director* for management advice. She bought a stretch of land next to Ocean View, and the Madeline Morton—her maiden name— Annex is now under construction. I hear she plans to move the health clinic into the new building, as well as a full-service legal clinic. And guess who will be running that? Counselor Mindy Johnson.

Destiny weaves a complex and beautiful tapestry. Mindy presented Maddie with her future on a silver platter, and Maddie in turn set Mindy on the noble path she yearned to find. And I hear rumblings about Maddie enjoying the company of a Brazilian mining tycoon on a rather frequent basis.

I want to believe that the first half of life is when you make your biggest mistakes. You learn the lessons, and you pay your dues. The second half is when you apply what you've learned, try to pass on wisdom to the next generation, decide what your legacy will be, and exhale. I have decided that mine will not be a legacy of isolation.

This is my second wind of the race and the skies are much clearer. It's time to enjoy and pamper myself, to let go of past tumbles, let people in, and receive all that life offers. I still make mistakes, I still say the wrong thing, my fears paralyze me, and at times, I let guilt get the best of me. But I'm working on it.

About the Author

From the age of three, B.B. Free always had a book on her nightstand, and so began her love affair with language. As a teenager, poetry became her favorite vehicle for expressing the rollercoaster of those angst-filled years. When she became an elementary school teacher, she discovered the range and quality of children's books and began creating thought-provoking storylines appropriate for children six to eleven. This is when *The Rescuers* was born, her first published work and a South Florida Writers Association award-winning story, which will also be published in Spanish. Her passion for writing soon expanded to include adult fiction and non-fiction. In 2016, she received the Cisco Writers Club Fiction Award for an excerpt from *Friends of the Bride.*

B.B. Free is married and has raised a daughter, now 29. She continues to teach and foster the love of reading in young children. She also writes a food blog where she chronicles her adventures in pursuing other passions… travel and fine dining!

You can find B.B. Free at:
www.facebook.com/bbfree61
www.goodreads.com/bbfree61
bbfree61.blogspot.com
Instagram@bbfree61

Thanks for reading. Please consider leaving an honest review on Amazon, Barnes & Noble, or Goodreads.

www.ingramcontent.com/pod-product-compliance
Lightning Source LLC
Chambersburg PA
CBHW020546120726
47903CB00001B/157